FACING DOWN

the TOUGH STUFF

Karen Dockrey
with Kathryn Templeton, Emily Dockrey, Andrew
Adams, and Beth Matthews

Chariot Victor Publishing
A Division of Cook Communications

Chariot Victor Publishing
A division of Cook Communications, Colorado Springs, CO 80918
Cook Communications, Paris, Ontario
Kingsway Communications, Eastbourne, England

FACING DOWN THE TOUGH STUFF
© 1998 by Karen Dockrey

Unless otherwise noted, Scripture quotations in this publication are from the *Holy
Bible, New International Version.* Copyright ©1973, 1978, 1984, International
Bible Society. Used by permission of Zondervan Publishing House. All rights
reserved. Verses marked (GNB) are from the *Good News Bible*—Old Testament: ©
American Bible Society1976; New Testament: © American Bible Society 1966,
1971, 1976.

Designed by Andrea Boven
Edited by LoraBeth Norton and Jane Vogel
First printing, 1998
02 01 00 99 98   5 4 3 2 1

Facing Down the Tough Stuff

Join Kathryn, Emily, Anna, Brian, Rachel, Ben, and Elizabeth as they tell you about tough stuff kids face and how God helps them with it. Accept their invitation to walk along and be the friend who faces tough stuff with them. As a trio you, your friend, and God can face down the tough stuff this world delivers.

TABLE OF CONTENTS

1. *Face Down the Tough Stuff Together* 7

2. *There's More Than One Way to Be Smart*
      A Real-Life Story by Someone Like You 11

3. *Find Tools to Face Down the Tough Stuff* 31

4. *You'll Never Believe What They Told Me*
      A Real-Life Story by Someone Like You 35

5. *See Tough Stuff for What It Is* 57

6. *I Only See My Dad on Weekends*
      A Real-Life Dialogue with People Like You 61

7. *Make Caring Choices No Matter What* 83

8. *Where Did All My Friends Go?*
      A Real-Life Story by Someone Like You 89

   A Note to Parents, Teachers, and Caregivers 105

   Ideas for Group or Individual Study 109

FACE DOWN THE
TOUGH STUFF TOGETHER

You feel really sad.

Your friend struggles with a learning disability, and people call her a dummy.

A guy in your classroom is absent. They say he has cancer. Your neighbor died of cancer last year.

Will your friend die too?

A divorce is breaking the heart of your best friend.

The girl next to you in school is reeling from a former friend's announcement that she's no longer cool enough to sit at the lunch table.

You want to fix it all. To make the pain go away. Since you can't change it, there's nothing you can really do. Right?

Absolutely not.

There is always something you can do to help a friend through a hard time. You may be a kid, but you have power no adult can ever have. You can be the same-age friend who takes away the loneliness from the path your friend is walking. You can remind your friend that life can be good because the two of you will do things together. You can't fix the learning disability. You can't cure the cancer. You can't tell your friend's parents to stay together. You can't beat up the bullies who call themselves the popular crowd.

But you can walk along.

You can say the kind thing. Play a fun game. Or just sit next to your friend while he gets a shot. You can help your friend discover strategies that will make school, shots, sadness, and scorn manageable.

You can be the friend who shows that every person is smart, that a bald head doesn't get in the way of friendship, that tears of sadness over divorce and remarriage are okay, and that not all friends desert you.

Together you and your friend can face down the tough stuff.

The Bible says it like this:

> *Two are better than one, because they have a good return for*
> *their work;*
> *If one falls down, his friend can help him up.*
> *But pity the man who falls and has no one to help him up!. . .*
> *Though one may be overpowered, two can defend themselves.*
> *A cord of three strands is not quickly broken (Ecc. 4:9-10, 12).*

Together you and your friend are better than one. Together you can find actions and words that solve the struggles. You might say, "That's their loss" about the kids who snub your friend at the lunch table, then form a friendship that's so fun and natural that your friend feels less lonely for the others. Let your friendship group never do the same ugly action.

When your friends face tough stuff, don't pamper them or

baby them. That's pity. Instead treat them just like every-body else—invite your friend with cancer to your birthday party. Do homework with your friend with a learning dis-ability, teaching her what you know and inviting her to teach you what she knows. Just share life. That's what your friend going through tough stuff really wants—someone who will like him for who he is, not someone who feels sorry for him.

Be just as interested in your friend's ball game as you are in his blended family. Rather than assume your friend feels a certain way, say, "Tell me about it." Then really listen, and care about what your friend tells you. Avoid words suck as "So?" or "Could be worse!" Instead, hear how your friend feels and discover what the two of you might do to solve it. For example, your friend's new stepsibling might drive him crazy. Invite him to tell you what he has tried. Add things you've tried with the people who live in your house. Together find ways to manage the awkward newness.

The kids in this book will show you how to do all of this. Each story was written by at least one real kid, a kid just like you. Through their stories, they show you how to face down tough stuff with your friends. First meet Kathryn, the pen name for a tenth-grade Christian who likes to make people laugh. She is outgoing and friendly, easy to talk to, and not very shy. She plays soccer and tennis, and partici-pates in tons of school activities. She is a gifted artist and a delightful friend. Besides all this, she's wise in the ways that count.

THERE'S MORE THAN ONE WAY TO BE SMART

"How could he do such a thing!" I stormed. "It isn't right!"

"Take it easy, Kathryn, and tell me what happened," responded Mrs. Williams.

"First Mr. Hume gave us a meaningless art test that everybody fails. Then he asks why the whole class did so bad. He actually said, 'Raise your hand if you are in Resource. The rest of you should have passed with flying colors.' How dare he imply that we'd be dumb in art just because we go to special education classes for other subjects? Did it ever dawn on him that his test might be the thing that's stupid?"

"I agree," said Mrs. Williams. "It isn't right to say that."

Refuse the Labels

I'm Kathryn, and Mrs. Williams is my especially wonderful special-education teacher. We call special education "Resource" at my school. A resource class is for students who learn differently from most other students. There are resource classes for students who learn faster ("gifted") and for students who learn more slowly or with different methods ("learning disabled"). I go to one that gives help in math.

Lots of people think resource classes are "dumb" classes, but not Mrs. Williams. She treats me like a human being and values what I say. She doesn't always agree with me, but she always listens. And even when she disagrees, she takes me seriously.

Now she said, "I'll talk to Mr. Hume to hear his side of the story. And I'll remind him that none of you has a learning disability in art. I'm sorry."

"Me too," I agreed. "I just don't see why life has to be so hard for us."

"The fact is, life is hard for everybody. Your learning disability causes trouble for you. Other people's friends or families cause trouble. And some have physical problems or health problems," said Mrs. Williams.

"I know, I know," I said. "But it's still hard."

* * *

My learning disability is an auditory memory disability, which means I have trouble with memorizing and with math. "Auditory" sounds like hearing, but it has more to do with language. I make high grades in some subjects, so I'm not stupid. It just takes me a little longer on some things.

I don't mind talking about my learning disability, but I don't want everyone to know about it. Once some people hear the words "learning disability" they automatically assume I can't do anything. The other day, for example, I misspelled a word. That can happen to anyone, so I wasn't worried. But Taylor, my so-called good friend, laughed and said, "C'mon, Kathryn, don't be so stupid. No wonder you're in Resource."

Taylor and I have been good friends for a long time, and I know she didn't mean to hurt me. But it did hurt—especially since she said it so other people heard. I wondered if they would start thinking I'm dumb.

My other friends aren't that way. Kimberly was standing right there when Taylor said I was stupid. Later, when we were alone, Kimberly told me about times she had misspelled words. Kimberly, who is very smart in school and goes to the gifted class, always reminds me that I'm not dumb. She says it's the person, not the label that counts.

I agree. I hate being labeled. It's as though I'm canned food. Labels make people assume certain things. They think L.D. means stupid. Once some friends and I got tired of the label L.D. so we made up our own name. We started the R.A.S. club, for "Regular and Able Students." I liked that label better. But what I really want to be called is Kathryn.

I'm a person first. I want people to know I'm a committed Christian, an outgoing student, an easy-to-talk-to person. I like to make people laugh. I enjoy playing soccer and being involved in tons of school activities. Labels bother me because nobody will look past labels to get to know *me*. It's like I walk around with a purple dot in the middle of my forehead that blinks L.D.! L.D.! Some of my friends know about my learning disability and some don't. I don't make a point of telling them because I don't think it's the main thing about me.

Notice Why People Do the Stuff They Do

I told my mom what Taylor said. She suggested Taylor may have been using me to make herself feel better. That sounded weird at first, but then it began to make sense. Taylor has a learning disability too, and was in special education class until last year. She always had a different feeling about it, as though she thinks kids with L.D. are a lower class or something. Now that she's out of special education, she taunts the rest of us who are still in it.

I think my mom may be right. Taylor's using me to make herself feel smart. Her grades have been pretty bad this year. So she jumps at every chance to make me look dumb. This wasn't the first time she had called me stupid, and I was tired of it. I decided to talk to her.

"Okay, Taylor, the joke's over," I said. Then I poured out everything I'd been feeling. "I'm not stupid, and I don't appreciate you saying I am. Once or twice is bearable, but you've pushed it too far."

"I'm sorry, Kathryn. I was just joking around."

"It's not joking when you do it at my expense," I said. "I know you mean to be funny, but this is no laughing matter. Why do you say stuff like that about me, especially when people are listening?"

"It's just for fun! Can't you take a little joke?" she asked.

"Yes, I can take a joke, but this is no joke. You of all people ought to know how it feels to be in special education. I don't feel bad about being in that class, but I do feel bad about the way others react to it. You may be glad to be out of there, but leave the rest of us alone."

"You take things too seriously," said Taylor.

"Well, you need to take this more seriously," I said. "I don't hate your guts or anything. I'm just disappointed in you. You're supposed to be my friend. I don't want you to hurt me anymore."

She acted as though nothing I said had gotten through. I just had to hope it did. Later I learned that Kimberly talked to her too, explaining that her words had hurt me. Taylor just said, "It was no big deal. She can't take a little teasing."

Taylor never apologized, but a couple of weeks later I sat down next to her.

"Kathryn," she said, "I was wondering if you could help me study for the science quiz. I guess it's no secret that I haven't been doing too well in there."

"Sure, I'll help," I responded. Inwardly I was shocked. Taylor, who had made fun of me only the week before, was asking for my help! I wanted to say, "You want a dummy to help you?" but I held my tongue. I could tell she felt nervous.

Things didn't automatically get better. Taylor kept comparing herself to me, bragging about how she took smarter classes. Toward the end of the school year she started writing me nasty notes. In one note she called me an idiot and said it wasn't fair that I had good grades. Then next time she'd write something nice. Every time I'd decide to forgive and forget, she'd write something mean again. It was terrible.

My mom suggested we get someone to help us talk things through. She said when a third person explains the way you feel, it can help two people understand each other. That third person is called a mediator. Taylor and I asked the school counselor to be our mediator. It wasn't a war; we just wanted to work things out.

We showed her the notes we had been writing. She suggested that Taylor and I agree to stop exchanging notes, and we did.

With Taylor sitting right there, the counselor helped me understand why Taylor said mean things. Her parents called her an idiot when things went wrong, so Taylor did it to me. Her parents told her she couldn't do anything, so she began to believe she couldn't. No wonder she hated special education class so much.

With me sitting right there, the counselor helped Taylor understand special education. She said, "Taylor, you are wrong about Resource. The education that happens in that room is just as valuable as the education in any other class. You can't say that your class is more acceptable simply because it's not called a Resource class. You can't put Kathryn down just because you hate Resource."

That gave me courage to say, "Taylor, how would you feel if I kept saying I'm in a better class? I can't be your friend if you ride me about Resource. I'm not exactly thrilled to be in Resource class, but I'm certainly not ashamed of it. I don't mind humor, but I do mind being attacked. We've been friends for three years. I'd hate to throw it away."

Taylor gradually started acting better. Every now and then she puts in a jab, but I remind her to quit, and she does. We're going to camp together this summer.

Learning about Taylor's parents has made me really grateful for my own. My mom has always believed in me and pushed me to go on when things get hard. She helps me pick up the pieces and decide what to do next. She's always there to help me with my homework, to teach me a better way to remember, to help me solve my friendship problems. She helps me feel good about being me.

Find Tricks for Learning

I remember my mom helping me learn subtraction in third grade. Some days I'd get so frustrated I'd begin to shake and cry. Mom would pat me on the back and say, "Calm down, you can do it. You're going to have to go ahead and do this, so let's get at it. There are only three problems left."

And I would do it.

My mom pretty much taught me how to do math.

Because I can't remember math facts, she showed me how to figure them out. Like if I'm adding six plus six, there's a five in both sixes. That makes ten. Then I add on the two leftover ones to make twelve.

When I got to multiplication we learned another set of tricks. To multiply three times four, I add the first two threes to get six, then six plus three is nine, and then I go, "ten, eleven, twelve" to add the last three on.

I hate math because it's so hard for me. When I get stuck in it, I get really mad. Mom reminds me to ask her or my teacher right away when I get confused, even if I think my question is stupid. My mom's a teacher, so she knows what teachers are like. When I ask early, I usually don't get as frustrated as if I wait.

My dad's real supportive too. Because he can't be there right after school, he doesn't help as much with homework, but he finds other ways to support me. He tests me on my spelling words and asks how things are going. Once when I brought home an A on my report card, he called me a rocket scientist. Now, I'll never be a rocket scientist, but he made me feel like one! There was a D on that same report card, but he talked about the good grade.

My dad always encourages me to do my best. I know he really believes in me, and that helps so much. I can ask him for help whenever I need it. In seventh grade I was real behind because of a bad sixth-grade year, so dad got me a tutor. She helped a lot.

Go Ahead and Get Mad

I try to understand why Taylor and Mr. Hume act the way they do, but that doesn't mean I never get mad. Being mad helps me in two ways—it burns off the pain, and it gives me courage to ask people to change.

You know in the Bible it says to be angry, but don't sin? Well, if we never get mad, we aren't obeying the Bible very well! At the same time if we use our anger to hurt people, we sin. So I try to use mine in good ways, ways that get the wrong to stop, ways that heal both me and the person I'm angry with.

Sometimes I put my anger into humor. Every now and then a kid will walk by and peek in the special education room as if to discover what a Resource kid looks and acts like. That drives me crazy. It's as though they think we're from another planet or something. If I'm in a good mood I say, "Those kids are walking past our classroom and studying our species."

I joke about my L.D. a lot. If I do something wrong, I make a funny noise. People laugh at me and it distracts them from the mistake. Once when my longtime friend and I were in a crazy mood, we decided we had turtleitis— because we were thinking slowly that day. We planned to send our brains back to the factory along with a letter requesting a refund because they obviously forgot some parts. Some days we think fast. Some days we think slowly. But we always find a way to get done what needs doing. And we definitely don't think of ourselves as slow.

A true joke relieves the pain, instead of making it worse. A joke is never funny when it makes fun of someone, like when Taylor makes fun of me. When other people joke like that, I sometimes let it roll off my back. While heading for my classroom one day, I overheard some guy say he was going to get into an easy class like Resource. I felt like hitting him, but he's a snobby kid who lives in a fancy house, always gets his way, and doesn't work for anything. He makes fun of everybody and doesn't care how badly he hurts people. He's the type who's not worth responding to; he'd never understand anyway. So I ignored him.

But I can't always ignore it. Like once in my regular class we watched a movie about kids with learning disabilities. It was very truthful. It presented kids with learning disabilities as normal, everyday people. At lunch that day, a group of my friends made fun of retarded people. I just had to say something.

"I'm one of those people, and I don't appreciate what you're doing," I said.

"You're not retarded, Kathryn," said Seth, taken aback.

"No, I'm not retarded, but I do have trouble learning. I'm a person, just like you, and just like a retarded person," I said. "You have to look past the label to see the person. If you'd known about my learning disability first, we might never have become friends."

He just stood there open-mouthed.

Another time I mentioned that I was not doing well in math. We were trying something new and it was hard. My friend said, "How can you fail Resource math?"

I shot back, "Pardon me, it's at my level. Do you have a problem with that?"

It bugs me when people know so little about learning disabilities. Once in typing class some guys were making fun of a student who couldn't type. They said, "He must be dyslexic—he spells backwards and types upside down." Everybody was laughing. They used dyslexia like a bad word and made it sound like a big joke. It's anything but a joke.

It's not fair that kids who struggle get treatment like that. Nobody should be treated that way. People who joke like that shouldn't come to school anymore. It makes me furious!

Sometimes adults can be just as bad. My friend Anita plays in band. Once when the brass section fell behind, the band director said, "If you can't keep up, we'll have to move you to a Resource band." Comments like that have got to stop.

Refuse to Go It Alone

It really helps to remember I never have to manage life by myself. God goes with me through my learning disability and other parts of life. He says, "Trust in Me," so I do. He didn't give me this learning disability; He helps me manage it. God's on my side helping me with learning and other everyday things. He helps me make my decisions and shows interest in every little detail. I try to do things to serve God, not to please other people or myself.

The best part is, God gives me more than Himself. He weaves just the right combination of people to give me the support I need. My family's wonderful, but when a family isn't strong, God gives a stronger dose of teachers and friends. When friends fail me, family and teachers are there to comfort me. When one teacher misunderstands, there's always another teacher who can help. God always sends someone.

There are tons of people who help me. I've already told you how great my parents are. God also gave me friends like Anita and Kimberly. Anita and I have been in special education classes together since third grade. I don't know what I'd do without her. She's different from me—she withdraws or cries when learning gets frustrating; I say something funny, or get mad and then move on. She gets nervous if the class talks about L.D.; I feel calm. She gets quiet when people tease her about her L.D.; I let people know in no uncertain terms that they are hurting me or someone else, to stop it and never start again.

Even with all these differences, Anita and I have a bond that's uncanny. We react differently, but we understand each other. We know what learning frustration is, and we know how it feels to be set apart. We also know how to help each other. She struggles with English so I help her with that. She helps me in math. We decided that if we could put our two brains together, we'd be great in school! We also help each other with family problems and friend problems.

One night we talked about our experiences with learning disabilities. She said the first time she had to go to a different class she cried so much her mom had to come to comfort her. She didn't like being taken out of regular class. That's when I realized that other kids with L.D. have the same problems I have.

Some of my best friends are in my special education class, but not all. Kimberly, my very best friend, finds school easy. She tells me never to let anything stop me from doing what's good in life. She says I can accomplish anything I put my mind to.

"You have to try harder at school, but you're the most understanding and forgiving person in the world," she told me. "You've got more self-confidence than I do in sports and friendships. You never let criticism or challenges get in your way."

When someone believes in me that much, I can't help but succeed! She builds me up and I build her up. Kimberly hates to see me get hurt. If she hears people criticize special classes, she gives them a big lecture. She says, "They think other people are below them. They'll know what low really feels like after I tell them how ignorant they are. Anybody who makes fun of other people is the stupidest form of life."

I asked Kimberly how her being in gifted class and my being in L.D. class affects our relationship. It made me feel good when she said, "I can't remember when I first found out about it, but it didn't make any difference. We were already close friends. I didn't even know what L.D. was when I first heard about it. When we met, I could tell you had a lot of talent and were very smart. You are the most talented artist I know."

God has also given me some neat adult friends. I remember the day the special-education teacher came to my class to do testing. I was so scared, but she put me at ease. She has become one of my best grown-up friends. She has watched me grow and has been there for me as I go through things. She's like a second mom. She has taken me and other kids with L.D. on outings. She teaches me how to manage trouble, makes learning enjoyable, makes me feel capable, and pushes me on.

Mrs. Bowers is another favorite teacher. She treats me like I'm human. I can laugh with her, not just about L.D., but about lots of other stuff. She's the type of person who goes out of her way to make sure I understand without making me feel set apart or put on the spot.

I once had a teacher who kept asking me if I needed help. He tried to be subtle, but everybody kept saying, "What'd he say to you?" I wanted to sink into the floor. Mrs. Bowers isn't like that. She helps me learn, but treats me with great respect. We read hard books and everything. She's upbeat and interesting. She's always telling us what she likes about us, and that makes us want to do our best. She says I'm creative and a good person. It embarrasses me, but I love it.

There are also great people at church. I don't have to

worry about my learning disability there. Church gives me the same sort of secure feeling I felt in my elementary school special-education class: the teacher cares, and I don't have to explain to anybody. The preacher knows me, and our families are close. My learning disability is no big deal to him. He's always nice and understanding. I never feel like an outcast at church.

When my church teacher says, "Why don't you read these verses, Kathryn?" I may get tongue-tied, but others do too. I very rarely worry in church. If we're reading out of the Bible, I may not understand what's going on, but even the girl who's in the gifted class at school misses questions sometimes. We're all there to learn how to live the Bible. At church I feel like part of the team. God reminds me I'm not alone.

Be Smart

"Learning disabled" is not the same as dumb—after all, I'm writing this chapter! Learning disabled means you learn differently and certain kinds of learning are hard for you. But everyone can learn. I think it's really important to work for a good education and to be smart in ways that count.

Some people think kids with learning disabilities don't like learning or school. That may be true for some, but not me. I deeply want a good education, and I work really hard to get one. I try to get along with my teachers. I think they like the fact that I try my best, get my work in on time, and behave in class. I also try to make my papers as neat as I can. Then if I misspell a word or make a grammar mistake, they can tell that I tried my best. Most teachers are impressed by neatness.

When I struggle in school, God shows me where to go for

help or how to solve a situation for myself. He shows me I can be my own best friend by asking kindly for what I want or need. God never leaves me to go it alone.

One thing I particularly hate at school is how they put the troublemakers in my class. These kids want to cruise through school. When a kid in my school hauled off and hit a teacher, they put him in a Resource class. There's a big difference between a learning disability and refusing to behave. I think everybody's smart enough to behave.

We're also all smart enough to learn. All of us with learning disabilities can find strategies that help us learn. I keep my eyes on the teacher to understand what she is saying. When we read, I keep my finger on the spot where we left off. Then when the teacher comments, I don't lose my place in the book.

In math I concentrate hard, bring home what needs more work, ask lots of questions, and keep at it until I get it. I bring home notes for all my subjects, both notes I take and those I photocopy from friends. Then my parents can help me study it all. As soon as I get home I sit down right away to do my homework. If I feel like I'm not comprehending what we did in class, I go back and read the material again at home.

During tests I first answer the questions I know. Then I go back and work on the harder ones. If a teacher asks me something out loud that I don't know how to answer, I say, "Can you ask me that question a different way?"

I also need strategies to handle the disappointment and anger I face. Last week I took proficiencies—tests to make sure you know the basics of a subject. We could have as much time as we wanted, and I took four hours on the math part. I missed passing English by one lousy point and math by seven. I was so mad. I was also really sad. I worked my hardest and felt good about my efforts—but I didn't make it. I tried to tell myself I'd pass next time, because I came so close. But I was still really upset. I called my dad right when I got home and then talked to my mom. They think I'll pass next year, because I'll have learned more by then.*

Mrs. Bowers, my English teacher, said she'd come over and help me study next year. My teachers and parents won't let me stay down for long. Their listening and understanding help me handle my frustrations without exploding.

If I could, I'd whisk away my learning disability and make school instantly easy. But this is my life, and I've got to live it as best I can. I refuse to let my learning disability keep me from the good in life. I want to do it all: make the best grades I can, excel in sports and art, love my family and friends. God gave me life, and I'm going to enjoy it.

One way I do this is to pay attention to the good stuff that happens. Not all days are as hard as those I've described. Yesterday, for example, I got a 100 on a science quiz I didn't even study for. I also made an *A* on my science notebook. And I made a good grade on a test I had to pass to complete this six weeks. When things are calm, I forget I even have a learning disability. The other day a friend asked if I was in gifted classes! I loved that.

I try to think positively when something bad happens or when I'm facing a new challenge. When I walk into the classroom I try to have a positive attitude. If I tell myself I'll fail, I probably will. But if I tell myself it's just a test, I relax enough to do my best.

Sometimes I don't do great and I get discouraged. I just have to bring myself back up. God helps me with this. I just

* The next time Kathryn took her proficiencies, she passed them both!

think, *So I made a bad grade on the test. I'm not perfect.* I remind myself of God, my family, and my good friends who are always there. I remember I'm good at art and sports. I look at my successes and the good things that have happened.

Speaking of sports, I'm kind of lucky to be athletic. Many kids with L.D. are uncoordinated. I'm glad God gave me athletic and art ability. I like to create things, and I tremendously enjoy playing soccer, volleyball, and other sports.

I'm a Person Just Like You

I hate it when someone tells me I can't do something. One of my resource teachers said I couldn't go to college or I'd have to go to one with tutors. I don't want to get my outlook too high, but if can go to college, I want to find a way.*
Then again, I may need to set my sights on a trade school, maybe one for art. I love art. I might be able to find a school that doesn't require higher math courses. And I've also heard they have colleges with L.D. programs.

I want to make one thing really clear. I don't want to sail through school with no challenges. I want interesting assignments, and I want to be pushed. It bugs me that my teachers don't assign us any projects. Do they think we don't have the capability? That may be true for some, but not me. Projects are hands-on learning, and I want more of that. I know I'd learn better. Teachers seem to think I'll burst from the pressure if they assign me a science experiment or essay, but I'd like to try. I'd also like to dissect frogs and stuff like that.

I brought it up in class, and some of the other kids agreed with me. That made me feel really smart. I told Mrs.

*After high school Kathryn earned a scholarship and entered college.

Williams the school is there to work for us, not vice versa. True, some students are lazy. But what about those of us who want to learn? Maybe we can get science projects and hands-on learning. After all, that's how L.D. kids tend to learn best—with something we can see and touch.

Mrs. Williams once gave me a poetry assignment, and I loved it. What kids like us need is to be treated like normal students. We want all the interesting learning that other classes have. We want teachers to respect us as people, not as abnormalities, cases, inferior students, or as people who aren't capable of creative learning. When teachers respect us, we'll give it back. And when we respect teachers, they seem to respect us. We can work together.

I also think we should be able to be in clubs. All the "smarter" kids get into clubs that have to do with academics. I know we're not exactly the brains, but what about school stuff that deals with our level? Why aren't there clubs for us?

Learning disabilities don't mean we can't learn, but that we need to learn in different ways. I don't want people to make excuses for me or assume I can't do things. Instead I want them to teach in a way that makes sense to me. It seems like the best teachers teach the gifted classes, and those that teach in boring ways have the basic classes. I want to learn in all kinds of ways.

I wish all teachers understood L.D. better. Mrs. Williams thinks some teachers are almost scared of kids with L.D. We're not pieces of china. We just need to be shown how to learn. Teachers may have to adjust the way they teach a little, but we can work together to find out what's best. I don't mean to complain, but rather to make suggestions for getting even better. I have a lot of respect for teachers.

I also know there's more than one way to be smart. The

smartest people aren't those with the highest grades. They're the ones who obey God and who understand feelings. They're the ones who are friendly and enjoy life—I mean really enjoy it, not just brag or party.

My friend Kimberly is a great example. She gets me laughing whenever we're together. If I'm down, she helps me feel better. If I'm happy, she celebrates with me. I do the same thing for her.

The other day she called to me, "Have you tried out for select soccer yet?"

"Tryouts are tonight," I answered. "I've been practicing really hard, and I feel good about how I've been playing. I hope I make it!"

"You will," assured Kimberly. "My gymnastics meet is this weekend and I'm soooo nervous. Wish me luck!"

"Good luck!" I said as I hustled off to class.

I smiled as I realized that my very school-smart friend Kimberly needs me as much as I need her. That's what life is all about: walking on through the bad and enjoying the good. It's solving the problems so we can focus on the pleasures, encouraging each other every step of the way. Friendship, understanding, sharing life with people I care about. Those are the ways I really want to be smart.

Tools for the Tough Stuff

If you have a learning disability or know someone who does, these sources can answer your questions or direct you to someone who can:

• Talk with your special education supervisor: this person (or persons) works in your school system to make certain every student learns well. Call to ask questions and to get advice. Your school will have the phone number. Together you can find ways to learn well.

• Develop an I.E.P. These initials stand for Individualized Education Program. You, your parents, your teacher, your principal, and other representatives meet together to design an education program that helps you learn. This way everyone, including you, can understand and use learning strategies that enable you to succeed at school. Your I.E.P. might include methods for understanding, adaptations in testing, note-taking, whatever you need to learn the most. Children in the U.S. with learning disabilities are entitled to a free public-school education that matches their unique needs according to a federal law called Public Law 94-142. Your local school system or State Department of Education can tell you if you qualify for an I.E.P. and can explain how to develop one.

• Read books like *The School Survival Guide for Kids with LD: Ways to Make Learning Easier and More Fun* by Rhoda Cummings and Gary Fisher (Free Spirit Publishing, 400 First Avenue North, Minneapolis, MN, 55401). Through this book, people who have learning disabilities or who teach students with learning disabilities share their tips.

• Talk with caring teacher and your principal. Find educators who care about you and your learning. Build a team.

FIND TOOLS TO FACE
DOWN THE TOUGH STUFF

Notice what Kathryn has asked for. And notice what Emily asks for in the next story. They don't want pity or special treatment. They want you to like and enjoy them as friends.

They don't want you to freak out about learning disabilities or admire a fight with cancer. They want you to see this tough stuff as rotten obstacles they must work around to get on with the business of living. They don't want you to dwell on or to ignore their struggles. They want you to help them manage their tough stuff, and then move on to more fun pursuits. They want to help you with your tough stuff, and then move on to your fun stuff. They want the give and take of good friendship.

Kathryn, Emily, and any kid with tough stuff is more like you than different from you. Learning disabilities, cancer, blended-family struggles, and friendship squabbles are not the main thing about these kids. They're bothersome bumps on the road of life. Together you can drive over, around, or right through the center of them.

It's like opening a toolbox. You don't do all the repairing; nor do you let your friend do it all. You and your friend work as partners to fix the tough spots. You hand your friend one idea, and the next time she hands you one. You tinker with and readjust strategies until something works You choose the right tools at the right time to repair or move around evil. These tools include honest faith, shared togetherness, genuine understanding, talked-about questions, expressed emotions, and caring adults.

Kathryn's friends, teachers, and family gave her these tools and more:

- Her friend Kimberly gave her smartness—she reminded Kathryn that everyone makes mistakes, that understanding and confidence are the most important ways to be smart, that people who make fun of other people are the truly stupid, that friends can prompt each other to move past criticism and challenges.
- Her teacher Mrs. Williams gave her advocacy—she went to the rude teacher on Kathryn's behalf and showed Kathryn how to earn respect for herself.
- Her mom gave her tools for learning and urged her to be persistent.
- Her friend Kimberly gave her the tool of standing up with her. She talked to Taylor to convince her that it's never funny to make jokes about people.
- Her counselor served as mediator to help Kathryn and Taylor understand each other's points of view. She valued both girls so they could value each other.
- Her dad gave Kathryn the gift of believing in her when he called her a rocket scientist, noticing the *A* rather than the lower grades.
- Her friend Kimberly gave the gift of asking Kathryn's

help in sports and art.
- Several teachers gave her the security that freed her to learn.
- Her pastor and church friends helped her feel a part of the team.

Emily's friends and family also gave her tools of smartness, advocacy, persistence, standing up with her, and security. In addition:
- Doctors gave her a carefully evaluated chemotherapy protocol.
- Nurses spoke in pig Latin to make the painful procedures more bearable.
- Hospital friends found ways to make the waiting more like a party than a punishment.
- Church and school friends went with her to doctors' appointments.
- School friends prompted her to stay involved in school stuff to get her mind off the painful side effects of chemotherapy.
- One friend even decided to become an oncologist—a cancer doctor—to help with future cancer fights.

Could it be that most cancer doctors chose that profession because of a specific someone they wanted to help? This makes these doctors friends in the same way you are a friend by taking notes while Emily is away from class. Together you, the doctors, the nurses, and the parents make up a powerful cancer-fighting team. Let God guide you to add your tools to your friend's team.

Meet Emily, a sixth-grade Christian who loves to read, do crafts, and work jigsaw puzzles. She collects teddy bears and currently has over 100 of them, each different. Emily has written many stories, beginning with "Emily Tales" that she wrote at age four. She followed with an adventure series called The Blue Stone Chronicles and several other writings.

YOU'LL NEVER BELIEVE

WHAT THEY TOLD ME

I'm Emily, and from looking at me you'd think I was just a regular kid. I live with my mother, father, and sister. I have four best friends. My favorite food is pizza and my favorite Bible verse is Psalm 8:9. I like to stay up late, read, and make crafts. Pretty normal stuff. But there's something that makes me different from most kids. I had leukemia. It's a kind of cancer.

Now don't freak out or anything—I'm not planning on dying. It used to be that if you got leukemia, you died in a few months, but that's not always true any more. Now you can fight it with medicine. That's what I did . . . and I won.

When I was eight I started losing weight. I got sick a lot, and I felt tired all the time. My doctor said it was probably a growth spurt, that all my energy was going into growing instead of fighting illnesses.

But I kept getting sick. My fevers lasted a couple of weeks instead of a couple of days. I was pale and tired. I never felt good. Finally my mom took me to a different doctor. He did blood work and noticed that one of my blood counts was way too low. He sent us to the children's hospital for a bone-marrow test, which he said would tell us why the count was off.

When we walked into the hospital, everything smelled like rubbing alcohol. The doctors took blood out of my finger, examined me, and then started the bone marrow biopsy. My doctor had described it as "a shot in the back." I soon found out that it was much more than that! First they numbed my back. Then they put a needle in my hip bone to pull out some bone marrow. It felt like it was pulling my toes through my knees!

I didn't know the marrow would be liquid, but it looked like foamy blood. After the doctor checked it, he called me into a room. He told me I had leukemia. I just sat there calm as could be, swinging my legs over the table. Never once did I notice my parents' faces. If I had, they might have told me something.

What is leukemia? What does it mean? Those weren't exactly the questions I had when I first heard about this strange illness. I mean, I got sick a lot. Why was this any different? I'd miss a few days of school, take medicine, and get better, right? Wrong! Little did I know that one word I had never even heard before would have a much bigger impact on my life than just a couple of pill bottles.

How Long Did You Say This Illness Lasts?

The doctor told me I would have to stay in the hospital for a few days to start combination chemotherapy. Then I'd have to take chemotherapy for two years. I almost went crazy when I heard this! I'd never taken any medicine for two years. And chemotherapy sounded like some kind of torture. I soon discovered that combination chemotherapy (I call it chemo) is just a fancy word for lots of medicines working together. It's a way of fighting with chemicals rather than radiation or surgery. But I was right about one thing: Chemo is much rougher than the average medicine. Its side effects are definitely torture.

After my main doctor left, a surgeon came to tell me I'd have an operation to put a port-a-cath in my chest. A port-a-cath is a kind of built-in vein. I call it my port. It's about the width of a nickel with a long, thin tube attached to one side. This tube goes into a vein that leads to my heart. With a port, nurses can take blood and put in chemotherapy more easily because they don't have to search for a good vein. That means fewer needle sticks and less pain, which sounded good to me. Plus the surgeon promised me a TV in my room. And I knew God would be with me. I wasn't all that scared.

But then nurses brought me some books on cancer and orders for a chest x-ray. I asked why the books they brought were about cancer. They said, "Leukemia is a kind of cancer. It means your bone marrow isn't making the right kind of blood cells."

"How do you know I've got that?" I asked.

"When we looked at your bone marrow, all we saw were blasts, which means cancer cells. Instead of good healthy cells that do what blood is supposed to do, you have cancer cells," explained the nurse. "These cancer cells are immature and lazy blood cells that won't clot your blood, fight your infections, or carry oxygen. That's why you've been sick so much. We've got to stop the cancer cells from growing and start the right kind of blood cells growing instead."

"Oh," I said. By this time we'd been at the hospital all day, and I was really tired and hungry. We stopped on the way home for a tall lemonade and a roast beef sandwich. It tasted so good. Then all I wanted to do was lie down.

It's Easier to Read about Surgery

The next morning my mom woke me really early, and we drove to the hospital. My sister went to a friend's house until school. My dad went to work and planned to meet us at the hospital.

I wasn't allowed to eat anything at all. By the time we got to the hospital I was so tired that I had to lean on my mother. I thought I'd never take two steps, let alone make it all the way inside. I made myself comfortable on a couch while my parents filled out a bunch of papers.

They took me to a place where I changed into a hospital gown. Then I went to still another room where doctors and nurses asked me questions and took my blood pressure, temperature, and breathing rate, and tried to explain what was going to happen. None of it made much sense, because everything was happening at once!

Now I was getting scared. I had read tons of books about hospitals, so you'd think I'd be calm, but I was terrified about actually being in an operation. My main fear was that I would wake up while they were cutting. I don't know why I didn't just ask somebody about it, but I didn't. Weeks after my surgery, I finally asked and found out that there's a special person called an anesthesiologist who makes sure you stay asleep. That's all that person does. If only I'd asked sooner, I could have saved myself a load of worry!

My surgeon came out and wheeled me to the operating room. I had a choice of going to sleep with a mask or shot, and I chose the mask right away. I'd had enough shots the day before!

I woke up a couple of hours later. Some lady was trying to shove a board under my back. She wanted an x-ray of my new port, and I wasn't even awake yet!

After a while, a nurse I had met in the cancer clinic came in and took me to my room. My room had a color TV, and on my bed was a huge teddy bear. My mom and dad appeared a few minutes later. While they talked to the doctor, I drank a Coke and watched TV.

Then, like a swarm of flies, student doctors and nurses came in and poked and prodded and asked me questions. I was so tired I felt like screaming at them. But I stayed quiet. You can imagine my relief when they left.

I was really glad when lunch came, but I didn't stay glad for long. If you think school food is bad, you should try hospital food. When I lifted my tray lid I found limp green beans, a sorry-looking piece of chicken that tasted like last year's Thanksgiving turkey, some purplish beets, and a lump of something revolting. I think it was dessert.

That night it wasn't easy to sleep. I missed my own bed, and I was hooked up to an IV (that's short for intravenous tube for putting food or medicine directly into the bloodstream) that I had to be careful not to lie on. The second night was worse. It felt as though there was a knife in my chest where I'd had my surgery. I woke up a lot and was glad my dad was sleeping right in the room.

On my second day I spent most of the morning in the playroom. We made everything from shrinky dinks to key chains to macaroni necklaces. There were tons of games, a kid-size pool table, special visitors, people dressed up like Disney characters, puppets to work, and—best of all—two Nintendos.

After lunch my grandparents arrived. I was so glad to see them. Just then a nurse came in and said she had to give me a spinal tap. What a letdown! She started to explain what a spinal tap was, but I was so tired I couldn't understand. So there I was again not knowing what was in store.

We walked down the hall to another room. There I found out that a spinal tap is where a doctor or nurse sticks a very long needle into your spine while you're sitting Indian style and bending over into a ball. The only thing worse is a bone-marrow test.

The nurse explained why I would have to have spinals regularly. Leukemia cells like to hide in places where chemo can't get them. My brain and spinal cord are great hiding places; while the blood-brain barrier (a neat thing God gave us to protect our brains) keeps the chemo out, the leukemia cells are little enough to slip in. So we put chemotherapy right into my spine. That outsmarts those cancer cells. The nurse takes a little spinal fluid out first to make sure no leukemia cells have made their way there. Then they replace that fluid with medicine.

My parents were really glad to hear there was no leukemia in my spinal fluid. But all I could think about was how much my back hurt.

I've heard that some people think more about God when they're in pain or sick. But during pain I don't think about God any differently than at other times. I just feel sick. God is always with me, and I know He didn't give me the cancer, so our relationship goes on as good as usual. During the hard times I have so little energy that I just kind of lean on Him without really putting words to my prayers.

Over the next few days in the hospital I dragged my IV pole around, had a series of shots, and took a bunch of pills. That was the start of my chemotherapy.

In the evenings I liked reading in my bed. Reading made it easier to forget most of the pain. I could get totally into the book. I also liked to watch movies with my dad or play Uno with my mom. While falling asleep I listened to Christian music. Steven Curtis Chapman was, and still is, my favorite.

I had plenty of visitors, and people sent me lots of presents and cards. The people from my dad's office sent me a bag of things to do. My mom's coworkers sent me a big bunch of balloons. Once a boy who worked in the hospital came to the door and said, "Is this Emily Dockrey's room?" We said yes, and he started laughing. Then he brought in tons, and I mean tons, of balloons, flowers, candy, and toys. I counted my helium balloons, and I had sixty-five!

My fever came down as soon as I started the chemotherapy. And I had no dangerous reactions to it, so my doctor said I could go home at the end of the week. I was so glad to get away from the hospital. I could hardly wait to get into my own bed and sleep all night without the "beep-beep! beep-beep!" of my IV pole. When I got home, I put on my favorite pajamas and went straight to bed. Before I could even look at all of my helium balloons, I was out.

The Hardest Part of the Fight

After I got out of the hospital I stayed home for two weeks to be sure my blood counts stayed high enough to fight any illnesses I might pick up at school or church. You see, chemo drives down healthy blood counts as it attacks cancer cells. So it's easier to get sick, and harder to get well. Staying home wasn't that fun because I missed my friends and I felt rotten.

One of the first people to come see me was my friend Amanda.

"You'll never believe what I've got," I said. "Remember

last weekend I told you I was going to the doctor on Monday? Mom had warned me I might have a shot or two. Well, I ended up with a million, plus a chest x-ray. They took blood from my finger and arm, and marrow from my hip bone."

"What's marrow, and why in the world did they need that?" asked Amanda.

"Bone marrow is the stuff in the middle of your bones that makes your blood. I have a disease called leukemia that means my bone marrow isn't making blood right," I explained. "It's a kind of cancer."

"Cancer! Are you going to die?" asked Amanda, rather shakily.

"I'm not planning on it. If I don't take medicine called chemotherapy, I'll be dead in about six months. But I'm going to take it to get rid of the cancer."

"My first cat died of leukemia," Amanda said.

"Yeah, but cat leukemia and people leukemia are different. People used to die from leukemia all the time, but they've discovered drugs that can cure it," I said.

"How did you get it?" asked Amanda.

"I don't know. Neither do the doctors. It just happens. I think pollution does it," I said. "But don't worry, you can't catch it from me."

Amanda and other people had lots of questions, but I never really had that many. I knew this illness was just something I had to get through, like anything else. I saw it as a tunnel to go through, not a brick wall that would stop my life.

My mom and I talked a lot about heaven, but I didn't plan to go there for a long time. While I was in the hospital, an adult friend introduced me to a twenty-two year old named Charlotte. She's twenty-five now and was diagnosed with cancer when she was eight, just like me. Neither of us ever worried about dying. We just planned to live. We're still living and we're still good friends.

When I went back to school, I asked one of the nurses from the cancer clinic to come talk to my class. She told my friends all about leukemia, what I'd been through, what I'd go through next. She answered questions. Then everyone understood, and things went smoothly. Nobody was ever mean to me, even when my hair came out. Once when a guy said I couldn't wear a hat to school, my friends got after him and told him why I was wearing it. I never had to defend myself. My friends kept treating me just like everybody else. That's the way I like it.

I was also glad to get back to church. The Sunday before I went to the hospital we had begun a month-long Bible game, and my partner and I were ahead. I knew he'd be glad to see me back. When I got home, I wrote on the flap of my Bible, "Dear God, Please help me get over leukemia."

Those first few weeks were the hardest. After my hospital visit, I did the rest of my chemotherapy as an outpatient, meaning I didn't have to stay overnight in the hospital. I took lots of pills at home every day, and on Wednesdays went to a place in the hospital called the clinic. I had blood tests, medicine through my port, and medicine in my leg. I also had to bring home two leg-shots-to-go.

I kept the leg shots in my refrigerator to take to my local doctor's office—not very appetizing when you're looking for munchies. Twice a week I stopped by the doctor's office on the way to school with one of my shots-to-go. It was not my favorite way to start the day. That medicine had to go into a muscle in my leg. My nurse let me numb my leg with ice before she gave the shot. After nine leg shots I started weekly spinals—one thrill replaced by another!

Wednesdays were the worst because I went to clinic, took more pills, and got stuck more often. Once I had to have "the works," as one of my nurses called it: a bone marrow, a spinal, a port shot, and a leg-stick all in one day. Yuck!

Whenever somebody brought me a present, we put it in the present box. Then I'd choose a gift from the box before leaving for clinic, to open after the shots were over. I also took my diary along and wrote about what happened and how I felt about it. My grandmother gave me the diary right after I got diagnosed.

The first weeks were hard, not just because of the shots and pills, but because of what the shots and pills did to me. Chemo felt worse than the cancer ever did. One medicine made me lose my hair and made my legs hurt like crazy. Another medicine made me swell up like a chipmunk. That medicine doesn't mix with salt very well, so I had to go with very little salt for six weeks. That meant giving up most of the foods I liked: ham, potato chips, pretzels, pepperoni pizza. And all the medicines affected my emotions as well as my body. I felt rotten. I just kept hoping the cancer felt just as bad—so bad that it would die and never come back.

The routine I've been describing was my protocol, or schedule of treatment. Every kid who has cancer gets one. It tells what medicines to take when. Doctors have discovered some drugs work well together and some don't, some drugs are better early and some later, and some are better for certain cancers.

After four weeks I got the good news that my cancer had gone into remission. Remission means the doctors can't find any cancer. That's good, but it's not the end, because cancer can hide and come back. To keep the cancer from starting again, you have to keep taking chemo awhile.

The final stage of chemo is called maintenance therapy—medicine to keep the cancer from coming back. Maintenance lasts two years for girls and three years for boys. I think this is because girls are stronger. My maintenance was daily pills at home plus going to clinic every four weeks for a pulse of medicine—some in my port, some by mouth, some by spine. Some visits weren't so bad; I'd just get blood drawn and get some medicine in my port. But every third visit was a spinal day. Those were the weeks I dreaded.

A Typical Clinic Week

I jolted awake and looked at the clock. Five A.M. My day had started. It was the fourth Wednesday, and that meant clinic day. I would get a spinal and a port shot. My mind told me it was dumb to worry until I got on the treatment table, that I should just go back to sleep until my alarm went off, but my churning stomach would not listen. Then I remembered that my friend Mary would be coming along. I quit worrying about the shots and started planning the day.

I got dressed and fixed my hair. Now that I was in maintenance my hair was growing back. It was nice to have enough to style again. Before chemo, my hair was straight as a stick, but now it was coming back curly. Curly hair was the one perk we found to chemo.

Mom picked up Mary on the way to the hospital. In the car we wrote mad libs, stories with words left out. Part of our story came out: "We hung the mistletoe on the anthill. Ben and Sally catapulted each other under it."

The closer we got to the hospital the more nervous I got. I acted silly because I was worried, but Mary didn't mind. She just joked along.

While Mom checked in, Mary and I staked out our spot in the waiting room. I got weighed and measured and had my blood taken. Mom went with me, and I had a gentle nurse so it wasn't bad. Mary could have come in, but she didn't want to see the needle. I understood. I didn't want to see the needle either.

We had to wait forever to get my blood work back, see the doctor, and get medicine. During that time Mary and I pulled out my clinic bag full of games and stuff. We greeted the other kids as they arrived for their appointments and started a game of Uno. Mary and I played as a team until the doctor called me. Then she played in my place until I returned. She took the place of whoever was in with the doctor, so the game could go on.

When my turn came, I teased the doctor and asked if he had an appointment. He acted like the patient while I pre-scribed 200 bone marrow tests, 84 spinals, 50 leg shots, 98 port sticks, and 1000 pills. I told him it would cost only $8 million and he would feel better in no time. He laughed and checked me over. As soon as he was done, I left the talking to Mom and returned to my friends.

While we waited for my medicine to come, Mary and I went to the cafeteria. I used to hit the cafeteria before seeing the doctor, until the time I ate a bunch of candy hearts. He had to check me twice before he realized the purple color in my throat wasn't some dreaded bacteria! After that, Mom always made me wait.

Knowing I had a spinal ahead made my favorite chips taste kind of cardboardy. Again, I acted kind of crazy, but Mary didn't let my nervousness bother her. We just kept playing cards.

They called me for my spinal, and I offered to give it to Mary. I couldn't believe she wouldn't take my present. After all, those spinals cost a lot of money. You'd think after having a dozen spinal taps that I would be used to them, but just seeing that treatment table made me want to run. I got up on the table, crossed my legs, and rolled over into position, using Mom for a pillow.

My nurse started talking pig Latin. "Ust-jay elax-ray, Emily-ay. Ry-tay eep-day eething-bray ike-lay ee-way aught-tay ou-yay." (Translation: "Just relax, Emily. Try deep breathing like we taught you.") The pig Latin made the process more fun. I deciphered what she was saying and tried to follow her instructions.

I was relaxed, and the needle was in. Out dripped the spinal fluid. The nurse needed three tubes of fluid. "Hurry," I silently urged it. After the third tube, my nurse said, "Ube-tay ee-thray. Ere-hay omes-cay uh-thay edicine-may." ("Tube three. Here comes the medicine.")

The medicine hurt when they put it in. I winced and then out came the needle. "All-ay un-day. Eautiful-bay ob-jay." ("All done. Beautiful job.")

Phew! It was over and I could sit up. I got my port medicine and fled that room. Twelve weeks ahead without spinals! Now I could really enjoy the games with Mary.

In addition to the medicines I got at the clinic, I had to take extra medicine by mouth for five days. These pills plus the medicine in my port and spine would drive my body, emotions, and mind crazy for a week. I wasn't looking forward to it. I hated the aftereffects almost as much as the painful treatments.

On the way home I was pretty quiet. Relief that it was over plus getting up so early had me pretty tired. Mary didn't make me talk. She just sat next to me while we listened to Steven Curtis Chapman. When we got to my house, we played piano duets. The music distracted me from the pain. I went to bed early that night and went back to school the next day. By the weekend my legs hurt like crazy and my stomach burned. I had hardly slept as the medicines had built up in my system. I felt awful. Like I said earlier, the medicines weren't too bad the day I got them. But they felt steadily worse for seven days. While the medicine attacked the cancer cells it also attacked me, making my joints hurt and threatening to push out every hair on my body.

Chemo goes after fast-growing cells. Cancer cells are fast-growing, but so is hair, and the chemo doesn't know the difference. Usually I lost just a little bit of hair during maintenance, but I was always scared I'd go bald again. Just about the time my hair would stop falling, I'd get more medicine and it would start tumbling again. Even reading reminded me of it, because hair would fall in my book as I read.

My family went off to a hotel for the weekend to help me take my mind off it, but it was back to school on Monday. Mary met me outside my classroom. She knew I wouldn't feel good, but she didn't worry about it. She didn't push me, but she also didn't let me stay on the sidelines and feel sorry for myself.

"C'mon, Emily. Be my partner for this science experiment," she urged.

While I worked on the experiment I almost forgot the pain in my legs.

After class, when the ache returned, Mary said, "C'mon, let's go talk to Erin."

I honestly don't know what I'd do without Mary. There's a verse in the Bible that says to put your love into action. Mary does that for me.

The Good That God Pokes In

Once those horrible seven-day chemo cycles were over, life returned to mostly normal for three weeks. I went to school, took piano lessons, played basketball, and did everything I would have done without cancer. My legs were weak most of the time, but I did my best. I got tired of taking pills, but they didn't hurt.

Cancer is rotten, and nothing changes that. But going through cancer isn't all bad. God pokes in some neat things along the way. One is friends. Waiting forever to see the doctor or to get chemotherapy gave me lots of time to make friends with other waiting kids. I met children with many different kinds of cancer. They almost all have to be cured the same way: chemotherapy or radiation or surgery. We could honestly say to each other, "I know what you're going through."

My friends and I called ourselves the Clinic Gang, and we had great parties. We had parties for birthdays, for holidays, and for non-holidays. There's always a good reason for a party. For anyone who finished chemo, we ordered pizza and had a BIG party. We brought games, word puzzles, and other fun stuff to help pass the time. We traded books, shared news from our schools, and just enjoyed each other. We live as much as two hours away from each other, so clinic was our only chance to get together.

We even made the checkups fun. Once my friend Melissa and I traded places to try to fool a student doctor. She pretended to be me and let him examine her part of the way. Then she giggled and said he'd better check out the real Emily. We also joke with and play tricks on our regular doctor.

God also gave me camp. The camp I go to is just for kids who have or have had cancer. It's like regular camp except there's a medicine bell before meals, and most people take medicine or get IV treatments while there. I've gone for three years and can go for three more. Then I can be a counselor.

Camp is great fun. Sometimes we toast marshmallows and make s'mores. We have scavenger hunts and carnivals and stuff like that. Once we rode in a hot-air balloon. Another time we rode in a famous singer's limousine. Each day is a different theme. One year the themes were all holidays: Christmas, Fourth of July, and stuff like that.

Some of my friends who had cancer in an arm or leg had to have it amputated. They now wear fake arms or legs, and they use them to play funny tricks at camp. Once my cabin mate put her fake arm hanging out of a sleeping bag. She put a long pillow inside and a wig at the top. Then she told the nurse to come quick because someone was sick. It was really funny. It really did look like someone was in that sleeping bag.

God's good gifts also come in the form of free tickets given to children's hospitals. Once we rode the General Jackson showboat. There was a big four-course meal on board, and my parents carefully prepared me for what fork to use and all that. I did great until my dad offered me a black olive. Have you ever tasted them? Don't! I about choked! It was hard to stay sophisticated after that!

One of the best free things was my wish from a group called Dreammakers; they "grant wishes" to kids with life-threatening illnesses. They're like those in fairy tales, except they really happen.

My first wish was to not have cancer or chemotherapy. Then I wished for world peace. But I had to come up with something people could do. I chose to go to Disney World. My family rode on an airplane, and everything looked like toys on a Monopoly board. We stayed in a duplex especially for kids on dream trips. Every day they left us a present in our rooms.

The restaurant looked like a gingerbread house made of candy. Inside were tables covered with real peppermints under glass. The game room had video games you didn't have to put quarters into, and there was a great playground. We saw the Magic Kingdom, EPCOT, MGM, Sea World, and Universal Studios. We went at Christmas, and the decorations were great. It was so wonderful that just saying thank you seemed wimpy.

Having a wish granted sounds great, and it was. But let me tell you, I'd give it up in a minute if I didn't have to have leukemia. That brings me to the best thing that God gives: normal everyday happy things like a loving family and good friends. Once, while sitting at lunch, my friends talked about how bad their homes were. I thought, "Wow, I'm lucky. My family is great. Thanks, God"—and I forgot all about having cancer.

Finding Life in the Midst of Pain

Even when I had cancer, I wanted to be treated the same as other people. I didn't mind the presents, but I did mind if friends or adults treated me differently. I didn't want to be seen as a hero or as courageous. I wanted people to notice other parts of me, not just the cancer part. I wanted to go to school and church, do stuff with my friends, and enjoy my family. So I did. I even got an award at school for having a good attitude. I was so surprised and happy.

My family helped with my cancer fight. We worked hundreds of puzzles, went places, talked a lot, and did other things to get through the chemo. Once, when my joints were hurting from the chemo, my mom and I started crazily singing songs from the hymnal. We spontaneously wrote new words to the tune of "Pass It On."

> I hate to take my pills. It makes my joints feel awful.
> The worst night is a Wednesday. I hate to come home after church.
> 'Cause then I have to take a hundred pills. I hate to do it.
> It makes me mad. It makes me sad.
> I'd love to pass it on.
>
> I wish for you, my devil, this agony that I've found.
> You can depend on it. It'll make you feel like you deserve.
> I'll shout it from the mountain top; I want my world to know,
> My chemo stinks, it is a jinx,
> I'd love to pass it on.
>
> I wish for you, vincristine, to leave my hair alone.
> I'm tired of it falling out. I'd like to keep some please.
> You can have a little bit; but just don't take it all.
> I don't want this cancer stuff,
> But leave my head alone.
>
> They tell me that these pills will take away my cancer.
> But it seems to me that they cause the problem.
> I know in my head this helps me, but my body says
> "Leave me alone, I wanna go home."
> I'd love to pass it on.

Your sister or brother might be jealous of your illness. My sister thought I was lucky because I got so many presents. No matter how often I explained that it wasn't fun to get all those shots and feel the effects of the medicine, she thought she was missing out. So I would bring her back something from the hospital cafeteria, and we let her go with us on days she didn't have school.

My sister also hurt along with me. When I got spinals, she cried too. And she worried. She said she was afraid she'd become an only child because I might die. I never heard my sister say this, but some sisters or brothers feel like it's their fault that their siblings got cancer. Maybe they got mad and wished you'd go away; then they think the illness is their wish coming true.

One of the worst things about serious illnesses is that people die from them. My good friend Kelly died during her leukemia. I miss her so much. After she died I wrote lots of poems about her, visited her family, and cried a lot. It's nice knowing somebody in heaven, but I wish she were still here. She helped me realize that not getting better doesn't mean God doesn't love you. It just means the illness is cruel. Nobody was more lovable and dedicated to God than Kelly.

God walked with her and walks with me. He also cries with me. I know what it means to walk through the valley of the shadow of death, like the Bible says. God doesn't like cancer. He doesn't give it. I don't understand why some people call it a blessing. One day God will wipe it out forever. I can hardly wait.

Some people say not to worry—that I won't have any more trouble with cancer because I have so many people praying for me. But my friend Kelly had lots of people praying for her too. I know God is the One who helped doctors find the medicines that help cure cancer. That's the blessing part, because without them I wouldn't be here today. But I also know that good Christian people still die young. Until we go to heaven, we live in an imperfect world. We do the best we can and look forward to the perfection ahead. The Bible says there will be no more death, sorrow, crying, or pain. God Himself will wipe away our tears.

While we wait to be reunited with our friends who die, we keep fighting cancer. I watched one friend after another finish chemo and live on. We celebrated each end-of-treatment with a big party.

Finally, two and a half years after starting chemotherapy, my last day of cancer treatment came. It was January 8, 1992. I was in the sixth grade. I had looked forward to this for so long. After blood work, a bone-marrow biopsy, and a spinal, my doctor came in and said, "It's a nice healthy marrow. Congratulations."

I asked for his pizza order and went to the waiting room to check with everyone else. We then proudly ordered ten pizzas. I loved riding up the elevator with all those pizza boxes. The whole hospital smelled great. I couldn't believe I was finally done. I wish we could have had a party like that for Kelly.

Three years after being diagnosed with cancer, I'm still pretty much a regular kid. I still live with my mother, father, and sister, and I still have four best friends. I like to swim, read, talk with my friends, and do just about everything I did before. I go back to clinic for regular checkups to make sure the leukemia doesn't try to come back. I see my clinic friends less and less as we spend more time outside the hospital than in.

I wanted to write about cancer so you could know what it was like from someone who had cancer, not someone who just interviewed people. Sometimes you see movies or read stories about cancer, and people courageously die at the end. But today most kids with cancer survive. And we enjoy life.

Tools for the Tough Stuff

If you have a life-threatening illness or know someone who does, these sources can answer your questions or direct you to someone who can.

• Get information and support. Call the toll-free directory (1-800-555-1212) to ask if there is an association or society to provide information, support, a newsletter, and materials for your chronic illness. Look up the specific name in the white pages of your phone book for local chapters. Your doctor or other health-care professional can tell you about groups that specifically relate to your illness. Samples of both national and local groups include the American Cancer Society, the American Diabetes Association, the Alexander Graham Bell Association (for deaf and hard-of-hearing), the American Heart Association, the Arthritis Foundation, the Cystic Fibrosis Foundation, the Epilepsy Foundation of America, the Leukemia Society, the Little People's Society of America (for short-statured persons), the Lupus Foundation of America, the National Kidney Foundation, the Spina Bifida Association, and United Cerebral Palsy.

• Request EMLA(r)r. This by-prescription-only creme numbs skin so you can't feel injections. Emily would have loved to have had it during blood draws, bone-marrow tests, and spinal taps.

• Find friends who are going through the same type of health challenge. Get to know people in the waiting room. If you have a regular appointment, you may see the same friends every time. If not, your doctor or nurse can put you in touch with someone about your age who shares the same health struggle.

• Listen to songs. Christian songs not necessarily related to your illness can help by just making you feel happy. "Friends of the Family" is a cassette tape that expresses feelings kids have about going to the hospital or doctor. It's available from Celebration Shop, Inc., P.O. Box 355, Bedford, TX 76095. (817) 268-0020.

• Read *I Want to Grow Hair, I Want to Grow Up, I Want to Go to Boise* by Erma Bombeck (Harper & Row Publishers, 1989). It's about children surviving cancer. The pictures are as wonderful as the stories.

• Read *How It Feels to Fight for Your Life* (Little, Brown, and Company, 1989) and *How It Feels to Live with a Physical Disability* (Simon and Schuster, 1992), both by Jill Krementz. In these books, children share their stories of finding life and happiness in the midst of serious illness and disabilities.

SEE TOUGH STUFF FOR
WHAT IT IS

Sometimes when friends read a story by a kid like Emily, they admire her. They believe she has special courage or has been chosen by God to inspire others with her cancer fight. But friends going through tough stuff are not heroes or special Christians chosen to suffer. They are real kids who have encountered an evil section of this world. They know God would not give cancer to them. They hate the awful things they're going through. Like God, they are willing to call good stuff good, and evil stuff terrible.

Tough stuff is not good stuff. Tough stuff comes from this very imperfect world, one where brains don't work as God created them to work, where cells distort to hurt bodies rather than help, where people don't get the skills they need to build family relationships, and where peers choose to hurt rather than enjoy each other. The Bible assures us that "God is light; in him there is no darkness at all" (1 John 1:5). Also the Bible says this about God: "Which of you, if his son asks . . . for a fish, will give him a snake? If you then, though you are evil, know how to give good gifts to your children, how much more will your Father in heaven give good gifts to those who ask him!" (Matt. 7:9-11). Because God didn't give tough stuff to us, we can turn to him for help with these problems.

Courage is choosing to climb a mountain or do the right thing no matter what the opposition. Cancer does not give courage or any other good—it steals. Cancer steals energy, time, and often lives.

So instead of admiring Emily, fight the good fight with her.

Never tell a friend going through tough stuff that her difficulty was given to her by God. Who then can she turn to for help with it? Never tell a friend that her difficulty was given because she was extra good or extra bad. The Bible says that the rain falls on the good and bad alike (Matt. 5:45). The Bible shows us that God doesn't give His children "gifts" like cancer and divorce. Instead, He gives them gifts like friendship, power, medicine, relationship strategies, and understanding. He helps them fight bad things when they come along.

Cancer hurts the healthy bodies God wants. Learning disabilities confuse the way God designed our minds to work. Divorce and death bring sadness rather than togetherness. Friend troubles happen when people choose selfishness rather than love. All these products of our imperfect world hurt people and hurt God. Join God's forces against them. None of the tough stuff is the way God meant things to be. But tough stuff is the way things are in this world right now.

We can fight tough stuff with God's power. Bible verses such as Romans 8:21 and Revelation 21:4 remind us that one day the tough stuff will end. God will get rid of the evil and wipe away the pain evil has caused. But until that day, you and your friends need each other to make it through the tough stuff.

Rather than call hurting friends special, call them by name. Rather than treat your struggling friends with kid gloves, expect all the kindness and fun you'd expect from any other friend.

As you and your friends fight tough stuff, recognize that tough stuff is as different as kids. Not every child who fights cancer fights leukemia. And not every child who fights leukemia has the same treatment plan. Each set of tough stuff will have details of its own. So how can you understand?

Ask.

How can you know how to help?

Respond to the details you hear.

Invite parents, doctors, nurses, books, and your friends to teach you what to do. Together find God's personalized plan for responding to just the details of your friend's situation. Not everyone will speak as forthrightly as Kathryn, or face pain in the same way as Emily. But notice common threads that link all tough circumstances together:

- "I want to talk about it."
- "My feelings are powerful—and sometimes scary. Will you show me what to do with these feelings?"
- "I want you to help me."
- "I want you to go with me."
- "I want you to like me as a friend and do the other stuff of life with me too."

As you read the four stories in this book, invite God to guide you to kids in similar circumstances, kids who will walk more effectively through their crises because they have a friend like you. Kids going through tough stuff could be your best friend or someone you barely know. But in each case you can choose the friendship moves that make the tough stuff bearable.

The next story has two authors, both of whom live in blended families. They created the characters from their own experiences and the experiences of friends because they know God is the one who can show us how to create happy families. One author is a tenth-grade Christian who likes to make friends with people of all ages, likes sports of all kinds, and is very committed to God and his church. The other author is an eleventh-grade Christian with an adventuresome spirit and a contagious smile. She's the kind of person who makes you glad to be alive.

I ONLY SEE MY DAD

ON WEEKENDS

"Sometimes I wonder if my stepdad and I will ever get along," confided Anna. "We hardly say two words to each other. I'd like to talk to him about things, but he's really quiet. Then on days he does talk, he seems to want me to listen and not do any of the talking. If I say anything, he gets quiet again. I'm really not trying to cause a problem; I just want him to know my ideas. I guess we don't have enough in common."

"I think you should keep trying to talk to him," Brian answered. "But it's not easy to do. My stepmom and I don't often see eye to eye on things."

"It's different in my family," said Rachel. "It's my stepmom I can talk to easily. My mom and I don't get along. My stepmom and I can argue and still be close. She understands I'm just expressing my opinion, not trying to start World War III."

"Yeah," said Ben. "When I argue with my stepmom, she's like a real parent. I can give my opinion and she gives hers.

Even when we disagree, I treat her like she's right so I can hear her side of the story. We both go away happy."

Are all stepparents big bad meanies? Not at all. As these kids have said, parents are easy or hard to get along with depending on how parents choose to treat their kids—and on how the kids choose to treat the parents. Understanding and care work whether you have two, three, or four parents. Anna, Brian, Rachel, and Ben get along really well with some of their parents, not so well with others. This has more to do with the parents' choices than if there's a "step" in their name.

The four kids in this story are kids who love God and who live in blended families. A blended family means the parents have divorced or died, and at least one parent has married another person who may or may not have kids. We have asked Anna, Brian, Rachel, and Ben to introduce themselves and tell you their stories. They have different family experiences but have discovered four important truths:

(1) divorce is painful;

(2) blended families feel weird, at least for a little while;

(3) you can create happiness in a blended family;

(4) God is the only One who can give security during divorce and new-family blending.

Your Story Matters to God

I'm Anna and I have four parents, two sisters, a half brother, and a half sister. "Half" means they're my dad's kids, but not my mom's. They'd be "step" if they were neither my dad's or mom's kids, but my mom became their parent through marriage.

My stepdad married my mom and now lives with us and my two sisters. I see my dad, stepmom, and their two kids every other weekend, sometimes more.

I like to play the piano and watch basketball. My friends say they like my smile. I'm really active in my church group. When I get older I want to go on our church's mission trips; you have to be in ninth grade to do that. But I can do other neat stuff like teach in Bible school. I was really nervous the first time I taught. I thought my nervousness meant I didn't have enough faith, but my leader said being nervous can mean you take the job seriously. Bible school went great, and I was glad I didn't back out. For a long time I've wanted to be a teacher. I'm glad God gives me chances to learn how. I love little kids.

I'm Brian. I like all kinds of sports. This year I play basketball and baseball. My favorite subject is math. It's really fun. I have red hair and gray-green eyes. My parents divorced when I was three, so I don't remember much about it. I live with my mom and stepdad, their daughter, and my older brother.

My dad married Paula, and they stayed married a year, got divorced, remarried, and then divorced again. A few years later my dad met my current stepmom, and they've been married about five years.

I see my dad every other weekend, and he comes to all my ball games. When I'm at his house, I sleep in a big bedroom with my two stepbrothers, or I sleep in the living room. Home is where my mom and stepdad are. I go to church here, school here, and do most everything else here. In fact, even when I'm at my dad's for the weekend, he brings me back for school and church events.

I'm Rachel. The three things I like about myself are my naturally curly brown hair, my blue eyes, and my sense of humor.

I'm shy at first and then I talk so much you can't get a word in edgewise. I live with my dad, stepmom, a stepsister, and two half brothers. My mom never remarried. Some people think its strange that I'm a girl and I live with my dad. But that's the way it's been for as long as I can remember, so it seems normal to me. I'm glad God gave me my dad and stepmom. I don't see my mom much. She used to come for a week in summer, but she hasn't done that for a while.

I play in band at school. I like to make people happy by smiling at them or becoming friends with them. I also like to make people proud of me. I'm pretty laid back. One thing you might think strange is that I love cows—I mean, people take cows for granted. Just think of all the stuff they give us: milk, cheese, butter, something pretty to look at when you're driving. People think they're stupid animals. But they're wrong.

I'm Ben. I hate animal abuse. Some experimentation is okay, because if they hadn't tried medicines on animals first, most of us wouldn't be alive today. But trying make-up and doing painful experiments on them is stupid. Who needs makeup anyway? I live with my dad and stepmom. My mom married a different husband, and they live about an hour away. I see them most weekends, and I can call any-time. My stepdad had one kid when they married, and he's about my age. Then he and my mom had a son who's about two now.

I go to Morgan Middle School and make good grades (is that bragging?). I think making good grades is important because it means I can get into a better college and have more jobs to choose from. I go to church on Sundays and Wednesdays, and I try to make God happy by the way I act every day. I'm the only boy in my Sunday School class, but

I don't mind because there are lots of guys a year older or a year younger.

Your Connections Matter to God

"My parents divorced when I was seven," said Anna. "I remember it was hot when they separated, so it must have been summer. But they didn't divorce until March. Divorces must take a long time. My mom's second marriage was a year later. They didn't stay married long. Then she married my current stepdad."

"My dad got married four times, twice to the same person," said Brian.

"Some friends think parents are careless to marry so many people. It makes me feel bad when they say that. I think my mom just had bad luck," said Anna.

"Parents make mistakes just like anybody else," said Rachel. "I think a lot of it has to do with thinking you don't deserve better, so you settle for less than the best for you. My mom actually told my dad that he'd never get anybody better than her. He believed her and married her. I came along, and then Mom left."

"That's terrible!" sympathized Anna.

"Yeah," agreed Rachel. "I know it's not my fault, but I can't help feeling that if I'd been better in some way, they wouldn't have divorced."

"For me the divorce wasn't nearly as bad as the remarriage," said Brian. "When my dad started seeing the woman who became my stepmom, I didn't like her because she took time away from my dad and me. My dad and I are great friends as well as father and son. I like my stepmom now, but it took a while."

"I had a tough time liking my stepparent too, but for a

different reason," said Rachel. "When Dad and my step-mom married, I worried that their marriage would end up in divorce like my mom's and dad's. It took a long time to grow close to my stepmom. I didn't want to love her in case she didn't stay."

"When my mom and stepdad married, we moved to a new house. My grandfather, who had been living with us, moved to an apartment," explained Anna. "He didn't want my mom to marry my stepdad. About three months later he died. My sister Lindsay was crushed! We all were, but she was especially close to Grandfather and never got over it. She feels our stepdad killed Grandfather because he had to move out when our stepdad moved in."

"That must have been awful," said Ben.

"It was and is," said Anna. "It's made things really tense. I keep praying it will get better."

"I don't remember much about my parents' divorce or my dad's remarriage," said Ben. "He's been married to my stepmom for about nine years. Because I've lived with them all that time, it seems like home with her. She gives me per-mission and advice just like a regular parent. And like a regular parent, she likes to bug me. The other day she was acting crazy with a shampoo bottle. It was funny."

"I understand that my parents got divorced for the better. They fought a lot before they divorced," said Anna. "So things are much better in that respect. Also, my dad and stepmom have a little girl who is almost four and a little boy who is one. I love them so much. I feel as if they are my own brother and sister. If my parents had not gotten divorced I would have never had them."

"I bet it's easy to like them because they're little," said Ben. "My stepbrother and half brother get on my nerves. They're pretty bratty. They argue about everything and get

agreed Brian. "Like when my dad won't be real honest with my stepmom about how he feels."

"Do you say anything?" asked Rachel.

"When he and I are by ourselves I do. I say, 'Are you sure? Wouldn't it be better to talk it out rather than just give in?'" said Brian. "My dad and I understand each other because we're men. I don't like the way she controls him."

"My dad and I understand each other too," said Rachel. "But I'm no man!"

"Maybe it has more to do with personality," suggested Ben.

"I think it does," agreed Anna. "My dad has never been good at being a dad. He yells over dumb stuff, like if my stepmom's late or I can't find the hammer. He has the same problems with my half brother, so it's not a guy/girl thing."

"You must really hate your dad," said Rachel.

"No, I really don't," said Anna. "I love him a lot, and he loves me. He has good qualities. He just blows things out of proportion. He didn't have a loving family so he has a lot to overcome."

"My parents don't yell at each other or anything like that, but it's hard to go back and forth between houses," said Ben. "With my dad and stepmom, things are uniform and everything has a place and time. At my mom's, things are more relaxed."

"Sometimes I wish my family were normal: a mom, a dad, two kids. We would go places together, do things on weekends, and go to church on Sundays. When you have four parents, you have to work harder to please everyone," said Anna.

"Yeah," said Ben. "But in another sense my family with four parents is like a family with two parents. We all have problems. And we've all got to listen to God for help in solving them."

God Delights in Your Happy Times

"There are lots of good things about living in my blended family. In fact I can't think of anything really bad at my house. It's just like a normal home. My stepdad's just like a parent. I can honestly say I have three parents. My stepdad doesn't take my dad's place, but he loves me and takes care of me," said Brian.

"What about your stepmom?" said Anna.

"She still feels like a stepmom," said Brian.

"My stepdad feels like a stepdad—an extra adult I happen to know," said Ben. "But my stepmom feels like a mom. Maybe because I'm with her more."

"Some of the stuff that happens in blended families is normal stuff," explained Brian. "At my mom's house, the place I call home, I like to stay in my room a lot. My mom keeps asking what's wrong. I just want to be alone to think, that's all. I listen to the radio, do homework, stuff like that. My mom gets on my nerves when she keeps asking. But stuff like that happens in every family."

"Yeah, I like the regular stuff," said Anna. "My dad is really protective."

"My stepmom is so cool," said Rachel. "She's a great cook and will listen to me. She tells me how she handled things when she was a kid. She really understands, really knows how it feels. She does get mad about things, but I guess everybody does that sometimes."

"My mom is great too," said Anna. "I can't tell how many times she's saved me—once I needed a costume for a school play and I forgot to tell her. She stayed up all night making it and didn't get mad. Also, and this may sound really weird, she can really pack a suitcase. She always puts in just the things I need and want when I go to camp or somewhere like that. She knows what I like, and I love to go shopping with her. We're really close."

"One thing I like about our family is we can all laugh together," said Ben. "When one person is in a bad mood, the others cheer that one up."

"My dad's not real good at laughing and stuff like that," said Anna. "He doesn't listen very well either. But he does a lot of good things, and he's getting better at the listening part. Last night when we talked, we really seemed to understand each other. It was great."

"One thing good I can say about my stepmom is that she and my dad really know how to have fun," said Brian.

"My dad and stepmom are happy together," said Rachel. "Their relationship seems pretty good to me. Sometimes they argue, especially if one is tired or sad, but most of the time things are on a pretty even keel."

"I wish it were that way at my house," said Anna. "But my sisters and I get along really well. And my friends are great."

"I'm still me no matter what my family is like," said Brian. "It does get kind of complicated when something is going on at my mom's and it's supposed to be my weekend with my dad. Most of the time Dad is happy to take me though, even if it's a long drive."

"Or I just trade weekends," said Ben. "Usually that works out."

"There are a few advantages to having four parents. You get double birthdays, so more presents," said Brian. "And when one Christmas is over, there's still another to look forward to."

"We have to travel a lot to get both places on the same day or the same weekend," said Ben. "Or sometimes we switch. Like for Easter we go to my mom's parents one time and to my grandparents on my dad's side the next."

"And no matter what our family situation, God always

takes care of us. Even when a parent doesn't care or doesn't treat you right, God is there to give you security and love," said Anna.

"Yeah, being in a blended family is sort of like having hazel eyes," said Brian. "Some people have them, some don't. We still can do good stuff, be smart, have fun."

God Is with You Now and in the Future

"God makes a big difference in my family happiness," said Brian. "I remember coming home from school really upset when I was in sixth grade. I burst out crying and then asked God for peace. I just felt so calm. Now whenever I get uptight about anything, I ask God to calm me down."

"Yeah, it seems easier to handle everything with God," said Ben.

"God keeps me from cheating and reminds me to be honest when it would be easier to lie," said Rachel. "I want people to know they can trust me."

"And God helps me keep my cool in sports," said Brian. "Sometimes I have a really bad temper. God helps me with my temper at home too."

"Sometimes I don't do right with my praying, though," admitted Ben. "Like for a while at school I hadn't been getting my homework. I'd pray, 'Do something God, please!' and the teacher would put off turning in that assignment or say we could turn it in late for 10 percent off. That kind of praying won't work forever."

"That's kind of like using God, not loving Him," said Rachel.

"God's not just for the bad times. He makes the happy times happier too," added Anna. "I love church, even though none of my parents go. I wish they would go. My dad thinks church is dumb. He doesn't want to depend on anyone. Sometimes he criticizes me because I go to church. I wish he understood."

"I wish he did too," said Brian. "All four of my parents have been in church as long as I can remember. I've probably been going since before I was born."

"How'd you get in church, Anna, if your parents don't go?" asked Ben.

"My friend Amy invited me," said Anna. "We went to the same school. Now I go to a different school, but we're still great friends."

"My dad and stepmom are Christians and have been since they were my age," said Ben. "I've always known about and loved God, but I made my commitment public last year. My parents trust me because they know I'm a Christian and I won't do anything God wouldn't want me to do."

"My dad's a strong Christian," said Rachel. "My stepmom goes to church, but I don't know if she's a Christian yet. She doesn't say much about God. I became a Christian when I was eight. I like knowing God cares and has written me a letter called the Bible. I like the verse that says God knows everything I've been through, all my pain. It reminds me that God is not far from me."

"Yeah, sometimes I do feel like God is far away," agreed Anna. "But He's not. Psalm 139 is my favorite chapter. It says something like 'Search me, Lord. You created me. You know my every thought and feeling. You knit me together in my mother's womb.' That last part is my favorite because it shows I'm not junk."

"My favorite Bible verse is, 'Do unto others as you would have them do unto you,' " said Brian. "I'm usually a pretty nice guy to everybody, because I have no reason to be mean. Unless somebody's rude—then I tend to be rude."

"I like the verse about a friend sticking closer than a brother," said Ben.

"Yeah. Church is where my best friends are. Amy, Jenny, and I are almost inseparable," said Anna. "When they're around I never feel ugly or lonely."

"When sad things happen, our group of friends at church helps each other through. Melody has been through divorce and remarriage too. She's a real inspiration to me," said Rachel. "David's dad had an operation. And we were all excited when Barry made the track team. Good or bad, we do it together."

"But God doesn't stay at church," said Anna. "He goes with me to school. He gives me the courage to make new friends."

"God is always there for me. Even though my mom left, God will never divorce me," said Rachel.

"I'm counting on God to help me know how to love. Love confuses me," said Anna. "I think a lot of kids with divorced parents wonder what love is. I do. I don't understand how people are married until they die. I've never had that. Some of my friends' parents have always been married, and it's so weird to me."

"My friend's dad and stepmom are getting divorced," said Ben. "Though things seem pretty secure at my house, I wonder if divorce will happen again."

"I know what it's like to love a parent, sister, or friend, but what is it like to love a spouse for a lifetime?" asked Anna. "Each time my mom got married, she committed to love the man she married for life. But twice she divorced. Why?"

"Sometimes I wonder if I'll ever have love," said Rachel. "I'm scared to get into a relationship because I never want to get divorced."

"I guess in a way that's good because we'll work harder on marriage," said Anna. "I know that love takes work, and I won't take it for granted. I'll also watch carefully the kind of person I pick to marry. My youth leader said her parents didn't get along very well, and she had to work extra hard to build a good marriage. But she's succeeding. They're going on seventeen years now."

"My girlfriend and I have been dating for eight months," said Brian. "We get along great. The only thing that worries me is she can be really mean. She's never mean to me though."

"But couldn't she get mean if you married her?" said Anna. "Maybe she's just on her good behavior to impress you. I've heard you have to watch how they treat everybody, not just you."

"I don't think she'd ever treat me badly," said Brian.

"Anna may be right," said Ben. "My dad says my mom never raised her voice at him until about a year after they married. Then the yelling was awful. Looking back, he remembers that she used to yell at other people that way."

"My stepmom says love is something you choose, not something that happens or doesn't happen," said Rachel. "She always says, 'Choose to be kind, Rachel.'"

"If my parents had just been nice to each other in the first place, their love would have lasted. They wouldn't have divorced," said Anna. "I'm going to choose to be kind no matter how grouchy I feel. God is teaching me how."

"I'm going to learn from my parents' mistakes," said Ben. "I love my parents. Even though they're believers, they made some wrong choices and do a lot of wrong things. But I don't hate them for what they've done. I know I'll be tempted to make the same mistakes because that's what I grew up with. But with God's help I'll change."

"I know I can create a loving home and be a loving parent," said Rachel. "I'll choose to do that with God's help."

"Me too. I'm going to be careful about who I marry," said Ben. "Unless I see the girl God has for me, I'm just going to wait. Too many people don't wait. They take the first person who comes along."

"Or they stay with someone who doesn't treat them well. The Bible says we've got to love others as we love ourselves," said Brian. "If we don't like ourselves enough to stop wrong treatment, we can't love others very well."

"And if we don't believe we deserve a good marriage, we may not make one," said Anna. "I'm going to build a happy family because God made me good."

"I'm not going to get married early like my parents," said Brian. "My brother and his girlfriend have dated a year, and I can tell my parents are worried."

"I'm going to make sure I only date Christians," said Ben. "Then I won't find myself in love with a non-Christian."

"But just being a Christian isn't enough," said Brian. "Both my parents were Christians when they married, and they divorced."

"Well, yeah, but being a Christian is the first qualification on the list. Then I'll look for someone nice, someone I can talk to, and get along with," said Ben.

"Before I get married, I'm going to get a college education," said Anna. "Nobody in my family graduated from college except one cousin. So I'm planning on being one of the first ones to graduate. I want to be a teacher."

"And I want to be an author-illustrator," said Rachel.

"I don't really care what I do, but I want to enjoy my work," said Brian.

"I want to be happy and help others be happy, married or not," said Ben.

Our Advice to You

"If your family is going through divorce, find somebody to talk to," says Brian. "When you're all jumbled up inside, you need an outlet. Right now, my person is my mom. Your person might be your parents, a grandparent, a teacher, an adult at church. Just be sure to find somebody good. God will give you someone."

"Sometimes I talk to friends," adds Ben. "They don't always believe things are as bad as they are. When I tell them about things in my family, they say, 'That's normal.' But it's not normal for two people who loved each other once not to love each other now. And it's not normal for two people to fight a lot. So when you're talking to friends, don't try to convince them that things are normal when they're not. Accept things as they are."

"Don't blame yourself for your parents' divorce," urges Rachel. "It's not your fault that your parents have divorced and remarried. You had nothing to do with their decision. They divorced because of problems they chose not to resolve in their relationship. It's not something to do with you or the way you acted."

"It's hard to believe, but even parents have a lot of problems," Anna points out. "Especially when you're really small, you think parents are perfect. They're not. They make bad choices and do dumb things—sometimes that leads to divorce."

"Parents worry about the divorce too. They have a lot of sadness about it," agrees Rachel. "They worry about how it will affect you."

"They also worry about how they'll do things alone that they did together before—like pay the bills and make decisions," reminds Ben.

"And somebody has to move out and get another place

to live," Brian adds.

"When you're going through all this, it's a big help to turn to God," Anna says. "He knows exactly what you're going through. He knows your anger, your sadness, your fear. Talk to Him about all that. Read your Bible. It's a wonderful message from God."

"No matter how hard things seem to be, you'll get through it," assures Brian. "Keep the communication open between you and God, and between you and your parents. It will make things easier for all of you."

"Then be happy when things go well," adds Rachel. "And remember that God will never divorce you. He'll get you through no matter what people do to you. Not only will He get you through, He'll show you what to do about it."

Tools for the Tough Stuff

If you live in a blended family or know someone who does, these resources can help you build happiness in your family, answer your questions, or direct you to more help.

• Make friends with other families and stepfamilies. Because we learn how to get along by imitating others who get along, look around for blended and non-blended families in your church who seem very happy together. Watch and imitate the good things they do. All families can encourage each other. Ask their secrets to happiness. Ask your pastor to introduce you to similar families.

• Join a stepfamilies support group.

• Find information. The Stepfamily Association of America (215 Centennial Mall South, Suite 212, Lincoln, NE 68508) provides support and education for stepfamilies. Their newsletter, called *Stepfamilies*, offers relationship tips, problem-solving strategies, books and resources, research, and letters from other stepfamilies. The association also offers self-help books, membership, and support groups throughout the country. To order information or find a support group in your area, call 1-800-735-0329 or write to the address above.

• Read the Bible. Books such as Lamentations and Psalms can help when you're sad. Books such as Proverbs can give advice for everyday getting along.

• Read Christian books and magazines. *Growing a Family Where People Really Like Each Other* (Bethany, 1-800-328-6109) offers tips for getting along in your family, whether blended or not. Magazines such as *Brio* and *Campus Life* talk about real stuff real teenagers face.

• Keep a journal by writing down your feelings and experiences every day or two. Notice how God heals you and brings joy in your family.

MAKE CARING CHOICES
NO MATTER WHAT

Divorce is not the unpardonable sin. It involves real people who have made a series of sad choices that hurt other people. A husband chooses to give more attention to the newspaper than to the news his wife shares with him. The wife, rather than kindly asking her husband to put down the paper during supper so they can talk, gives him the silent treatment. Having seen his dad read the paper at supper, the husband makes no connection between her silence and his paper reading. He thinks she must be moody. She grows more irritated at his refusal to respond to her obvious displeasure. He has no clue why she's angry.

After a series of scenarios like this, the two drift apart. She stops even trying to share her ideas, feelings, and news. He reads more to escape the silence. They find the same frustration in other areas of their marriage. They decide maybe it would be better for everyone if they divorce. After all, they share no commonality.

Friendship is a series of choices too. Kenneth, eager to

share good news with his friend, bounds into school over-flowing. He starts to tell his story, only to be greeted with, "So?" Kenneth stops talking and walks dejectedly to his first class. There the boy across the aisle tells Kenneth how nervous he is about soccer tryouts and asks if Kenneth will pray for him. Still sad, Kenneth responds with a half-hearted, "Whatever." The soccer hopeful feels snubbed and rejected, confused by his usually enthusiastic friend's response.

Like ripples in a pond, each choice impacts the choices of many other people. Each word brings closeness or alienation. Each attitude makes the other more, or less, willing to work with you.

How much happier could the married couple have been if she had kindly said, "I really like hearing the events of your day and telling you mine. Can you read the paper after supper?"

What if the husband said, "Sure. You're more fun than a newspaper anyway!"

How might everyone's school day have been better if Kenneth's first friend had enthusiastically greeted his story with, "No kidding? Tell me more!" Or if Kenneth had told his soccer buddy that he wasn't feeling so happy at that moment and apologized for his half-hearted response.

You know all this, but you feel sappy if you show too much interest in people. Won't people think you're weird? The last time you tried caring like that, you got shot down. Aren't friends and spouses supposed to just know what the other person needs and wants?

Not at all.

It's complicated. But three things are certain: Sappy can be majorly cool when it means sincere interest shown in real people. Telling what you feel and need is much more effective than reading minds. God will equip you to care for your friends and family—you just have to choose to act.

So take the plunge. Be willing to learn relationship skills and to use them. Push aside worries over coolness or popularity so you can genuinely like the genuine people around you. That's real popularity.

Drop the mind-reading myth and choose to really communicate. Be willing to grow truly mature friendships— friendships that go much deeper than the second grade I-like-you-do-you-like-me? connections. It's the best part about middle school. You can build real friendships that last a lifetime.

It won't be easy. You'll feel like all eyes are on you. You'll worry that people think you're weird. But the truly cool people will notice you. And they'll like being with you.

Then one day, one of your opposite-sex friends will become your spouse. The friendship skills you've built over the years will give you a great foundation for marriage happiness. You'll spend your whole life with your best friend— a person you talk and listen to. The two of you will understand each other and work together well because you can say out loud what you need and want. Your comfort with each other will spill over onto your children so they can securely seek and make friends.

It's a tremendous goal. One that you grow closer to with each honest and caring action. Choose to show real care. Choose to really communicate. Learn from people who already do friendship and marriage well. Imitate them.

Then work in and around the imperfect circumstances that face you and your friends daily—friends who snub you rather than cherish you, parents who put their own needs ahead of their spouse's needs, and more. Don't condemn nor criticize. Talk. See yourselves as fellow strugglers on the road to learning to get along. Refuse to accept divorce and friendship division as the norm; instead work to build closeness so neither is necessary. Make your newly-blended family so close that no one will know that you haven't lived together all your lives. Treat each person at school with the attention and interest you love to receive. Affirm. Build up. Talk directly. Help with problems and then receive help. Such personalized care will stop the cycle of loneliness and put-downs that divide rather than unite.

Start where you are. Prompt each other to solve friendship and family problems rather than whining about them or pretending they don't matter. Move to greater understanding, steadier cooperation, and more persistent need-meeting. Find words and actions that treat people the same way Jesus would—even if that someone is a pesky younger stepsibling who drives you wild. God will show you, and your stepsibling, how.

None of us is born knowing how. We all have to learn relationship skills. Whether you were born to people who showed you how or not, you can grow your friendship and family skills. No matter what your circumstance, you can make caring choices. Think about how your family and friendships would be transformed if each of you consistently responded with kindness.

You and your friends can help each other through relationship tough stuff. Notice the ways Anna, Brian, Rachel, and Ben do that for each other. Then watch the way Elizabeth learns to move past her self-consciousness to build true friendships. Find actions that define what being a friend is all about—real love shown by real people in real life, because you really mean it. Put aside your fear and sadness so you can plunge right into caring.

The following friendship story has three authors: a sixth-grader, an eighth-grader, and a twelfth-grader. Together they created Elizabeth, a character who is a combination of all three. They give you a perspective on friendship that helps no matter what grade you're in. All three students are convinced that reaching outside yourself is the only way to build happy friendships.

WHERE DID ALL MY FRIENDS GO?

You can't find a good friend nowadays. In elementary school, friends were the ones who came to the clubs we invented on the playground. The only requirement was to check the yes box on the do-you-want-to-be-friends-forever note. But in middle school something weird started to happen. Talk turned ugly.

I'm Elizabeth, and the first thing that really ticks me off about friends and gets on my nerves big time is insults. I know just about everybody does it and doesn't seem to think it's a big deal, but I don't like it. I don't think it's very nice. It's mean. Friends are supposed to be our support group right? And they're supposed to help us through tough times, right? HA!

For instance, say I walk into school one morning and see my friends Teresa, Denise, Jessie, and Sandy. Now an ideal conversation should go something like this:

Me: "Hi, guys! Did you see The latest episode of __ last night? It was the best one yet!"

Teresa: "Yeah! Wasn't it great? It was so cool!"

Jessie: "You're right—that was the coolest episode!"

Sandy: "Oh I know! Wasn't it, though? I loved the part where he jumped off onto the train!"

Denise: "Guess what? I'm going to a gymnastics expedition today! I'm leaving at about 11:00"

Me: "I hope you do good!"

Teresa and Sandy in spontaneous unison: "Yeah, break a leg!"

Jessie: "I know you'll do great! We'll miss you."

Now wasn't that a great conversation? Everyone was NICE to each other! But here is a more realistic story:

Me: "Hey did you see the latest episode of __ last night?"

Teresa: "I can't believe you watch that! That's a little kids' show!"

Sandy: "You're such a loser to be watching that!"

Denise: "I'm going on a gymnastics expedition today!"

Jessie and Teresa: "Alleluia!"

Sandy: "Yea!"

Me: "Well, I'll miss you."

Sandy: "Don't lie like that!"

Me: "I'm not!"

Teresa: "Of course you are!"

Jessie: "I can't wait till she's gone!"

Now that was a little different. Unfortunately it's what happens every day in my middle school. Rather than caring about what people think, everybody puts down everybody else with every word out of their mouths.

Probably you've also experienced name-calling with words like "You're stupid!" "Dummy!" "Hey, loser!" "Whatever!" and, "You're a baby!"

But then it gets worse. Say you're playing Twenty Questions and guessing things during lunchtime at school:

Teresa: "Okay, go ahead and guess. I'll give you a hint. There are two of them and they're hairy and have four legs."

Denise: "A dog?"

Teresa: "Yes, but be more specific."

Jessie: "You and your sister!"

Teresa: "No."

Jessie: "Jan and Myra!"

Teresa: "Right!"

Denise: "I don't think that's funny!"

Jessie: "Yes it is!"

That's easy for Jessie to say. The joke isn't about her, you think to yourself. As you walk back to class your friends start another one:

Jessie: "Okay, I've got one! Guess! It's got four feet its furry and it's big."

Denise: "A dog?"

Jessie: "No."

Teresa: "A cat?"

Jessie: "No."

Teresa: "Denise!"

Me: "Did you say Denise?"

Jessie: "Never mind."

Teresa: "What?"

You feel anger building inside as you think, *Now that's bad! First they're calling each other dogs. Second of all Teresa acts like she doesn't know what she did. Or she thinks nothing is wrong with what she said. Oooooooohhhhhhhhhh!*

Okay, so now you've probably got a pretty good idea of what I'm talking about. I mean, who wants to walk into school when somebody shoots you down the first thing you say? It's almost like a you're a target sitting up there in the air waiting for someone to aim at you and hit you dead center in the bull's eye. This especially hurts when the shooter is your friend.

Now I know most of the time when people say ugly things, they follow it with, "Just kidding!" The problem is after a while it kind of starts to hit home and you start believing it. Picture this: Every day at school one or more of your friends tells you you're stupid for something you do. Or they criticize the way you look, what you like, or what you say. Well, soon you start wondering if you really are stupid. Or you wonder if your friends think you're stupid. When they say, "I'm kidding!" they might just be using that for an excuse.

I got really tired of all this. I prayed God would show me what to do. I prayed for friends.

Sweeping Changes

The problem had developed gradually. In elementary school we talked to everybody, made up playground clubs every week, and went to each other's birthday parties. But in middle school things changed. We still went to each other's birthday parties, but we started worrying about what was cool and what wasn't. We began to call people popular or not popular.

The ones who ended up worrying about popularity weren't the ones I expected to be that way. At the end of sixth grade Allie, my best friend from kindergarten and one of the nicest people you'd ever want to meet, started to turn her back on me when I talked to her. It was like she wasn't interested in what I had to say. I stayed quiet at first, but then decided to write her a note and tell her how her actions made me feel. Maybe she didn't realize what she was doing.

She apologized like crazy and then was super-sweet to me for about a week.

She wrote me notes just like old times, and she thanked me for writing her notes. She showed again the sensitivity that made me so crazy about her. I thought things were going to be fine. But she began writing me about her church and about wanting to get into the youth group and to go out with a guy. It sounded more and more like she was trying to do tenth-grade stuff when we were still in sixth grade.

After about three rounds of this talk-not talk-write a note-talk again, she quit talking to me altogether. Sometimes she'd talk to me if no one was close, but even then it was like she was looking over her shoulder to make sure she didn't get caught speaking to me. I'm just not cool enough for her. She wants to be in the popular crowd, and I'm not popular. So she snubs me.

This year she didn't invite me to her birthday party.

It hurts, but in one sense I'm relieved. Last year she acted so exclusive at my party that she almost ruined everything. She acted bored while we opened presents. She kept whispering to one or two people, and making the rest of us feel left out. It wasn't even her party or her house.

Little by little I've lost other friends too. Teresa and I met in the fourth grade and we got along great. She was new so I tried to make her feel at home. I'd wait for her and make sure she had a seat at the lunch table. We spent the night together, went on trips together, and laughed constantly. She never complained, even when we chose activities that weren't her favorites. She's one of the most adaptable people I know.

I always knew that if Teresa was there, I'd have someone to talk to.

Then about midway through this year, she and the rest of my lunch-table friends stopped saving a seat for me. When I asked if I could sit with them, they nonchalantly said there were no more chairs. I thought for a while it was an accident. But when it happened day after day, I realized I had been kicked out of the lunch table.

My mom offered to hang them by their toes, but I assured her I could handle it. I was glad that she cared enough to get mad. But it got old when she asked about the lunch table every single day. I wanted to just forget about it for a while.

I tried sitting at several other lunch tables, but I didn't feel very at home at any of them. So I tried going back to my old table. I got there early enough to get a seat. But no matter where I sat, somebody would come up and say that was her seat. My dad called them my fake friends. He suggested I get some real ones.

There was one girl, Dana, who had been pretty nice to me. She said that it was their loss for kicking me out of their table. That made me feel better. She acted like she really cared.

I kind of liked Dana, but she wasn't popular. Even as I thought that, I was ashamed of myself. I was doing just what Allie does. I was pushing away a totally nice person just because I'm worried about what other people think. But I didn't know how to get rid of the feeling.

Church Friends

My friends at church were also acting weird. I never quite knew what to expect. One week Karla would talk to me and the next she wouldn't. We had been friends since we were little girls. But now she was different. Trios were especially touchy. She and Jill would team up and talk only to each other. Or they'd both insult the rest of us. I tried to stay nice no matter how others acted, but it was hard.

I wanted to shout, "This is church! We should practice what we preach. Where is the love?" To be honest I wanted to say the same to Allie at school. She was a Christian, went to church all the time, and wore Christian T-shirts. But she treated people horribly—she wasn't mean just to me. I don't understand how she can say "Love your neighbor!" over and over and still act the way she does with a clear conscience.

But I didn't say that to Allie or any of my church friends.

And my parents made me keep on going to church, even when I felt left out.

One of our youth leaders had a no-insult rule that stopped some on the dog jokes and other insults. Slams still happened in the hall, but at least the classroom was safe. I tried to keep my words kind, but even I would slip into the people-slamming pattern every once in a while.

My senior high friend Faye says that treating people nicely will pay off. She says that after people get past middle school, most of them start to act like human beings again. And they'll remember how you treated them.

After several weeks, weeks that seemed like years, Karla began to notice how mean Jill treated her at church. Jill had been talking just as ugly to Karla as she had to everyone else, but I hadn't noticed. Jill loses her temper and yells. Karla told me last week that she's glad I'm not like that. I had to be really careful how I answered, because I didn't want to sound like I'm better than Jill.

I said, "Thanks. I know I wouldn't want to be treated that way."

"Me either. She makes me sick," said Karla.

I didn't know what to say because I didn't want to gossip about Jill. I was so happy that Karla was talking to me again and that our talk was real. She seemed to really care about what I said. But I didn't know how to answer this comment.

Just then Ann walked up. I pulled her into the conversation, changing the subject. She's not popular but I didn't want her to feel as left out as I'd been feeling. There I go again, calling people popular or not popular, just like I hate people doing to me.

Close Watching

As I fell asleep that night, thanking God for the breakthrough with Karla, my thoughts turned to Dana. I couldn't think of one time she had put me down or left me out. I liked that.

I started watching her more closely at school. We'd been friends for a while, but not what you'd call best friends. The more I was with Dana, the more I liked her.

While watching Dana, I also made friends with Sandy, one of the girls in the insult story I told you about earlier. Sandy was really popular, and my life at school got better after she and I became friends. Still, I felt lonely. That confused me. Here somebody popular was paying attention to me, but I still felt alone.

One thing I did understand was that I wasn't being myself. I did and said what Sandy wanted, not what I wanted. Even then she criticized me a lot. She criticized just about everybody. But I ignored it because I finally had someone at school I could call my good friend.

A few times while I was with Sandy I saw Dana. There

was something in her eyes. Something like anger. Something like sadness. Why was she mad? And why would someone as wonderful as Dana feel sad?

People started referring to Sandy and me as friends. *This is great!* I thought, *I finally have a popular friend.* But Sandy didn't seem to like it. She got really mysterious.

I felt very alone and very angry. I told myself that maybe I was imagining the whole thing. Then people started asking if Sandy was mad at me, or if I was mad at her. When I saw her talking with our friends, I walked up to join them. When she saw me, she'd roll her eyes and walk off. Once I tripped in the hall and my books went flying. Instead of helping me pick up everything, she said, "You are such an idiot! Can't you walk without falling on your face?"

I didn't like that much. She made me feel really stupid. I know I'm not stupid, but shouldn't Sandy know?

"No, Sandy doesn't know," explained my dad that night. "Sandy cares more about status than friendship. Who do you know who cares about friendship? About people?"

Dana came to mind. I didn't say anything. I just thought about her for a while.

I hadn't been ignoring Dana or anything. I just wasn't giving her my best time. I never really said or did anything mean to her. And I never insulted her. I just picked someone else if there was a choice.

No wonder Dana looked sad when I was with Sandy.

I began sitting at Dana's lunch table more. There was a difference in tone at that table. People still said insulting things. But the insults were occasional rather than constant. And people often apologized—"Oops. I shouldn't have said it that way."

Could Dana be the reason? People seemed to know she cared. I decided to have her over.

Real Fun

I've heard that people have fun in elementary school, stop having fun in middle school, and then start again in high school. I'm starting to believe it. We middle schoolers are so worried about being popular or cool that we won't do the things that are genuinely fun.

The interesting thing is that Dana didn't seem to care about that "rule."

When she came over we had an absolute blast. While looking through my room, we got into my closet and pulled out games I used to play when I was little. We got to talking about all the stuff we did when we were little kids.

"Oh, you used to watch "Sesame Street" too? I LOVED that show!"

"Big Bird was my favorite."

"I liked Elmo."

"Yeah. He was cool too."

"Did you ever play with ponies?"

"You played with ponies? Wasn't it fun to braid their tails!"

"And bike rides. We used to put sparkly things on the spokes that would click when we rode."

"That was great!"

"Hey. Do you have an extra bike?"

"I think we might. Why?"

"Let's go on a bike ride right now!"

So we did. I had to bite back feelings of *What if friends see us and think we're babies for riding bikes?* I reminded myself that anybody who worried about that just didn't know how to have fun.

The wind felt great in our hair. We raced and then coasted, taking time to talk along the way.

This is what friendship feels like, I recognized. Friendship is supposed to be fun and crazy times with people you really like, and who like you back. You relax with your friends.

So I said so. "Dana, I really like being with you. You're a great friend."

"Thanks. I like you, too."

"We're getting mushy, aren't we?" I asked.

"Mush is fine with me," Dana assured me. "We don't say often enough how we feel."

Surprise Discoveries

That night after Dana went home I realized I had hurt myself, Dana, and God by turning away from Dana to spend time with Sandy. The Bible says not to throw your pearls before pigs. That means we can't live the good that God has created in us if people step on it all the time. Just as pigs don't appreciate pearls, Sandy doesn't appreciate fun, kindness, love, honesty, and other true friendship qualities. It's not that Sandy is a bad person. It's that she's chosen to value surface stuff instead of the right stuff.

I had let Sandy, and others who treated me badly, step all over God's goodness. I had let these "friends" convince me I was a reject. I had let them push me to almost destroy a tremendous friendship, one like I'd dreamed about.

God had offered me friends, but I'd almost rejected them.

God had given me a lot to give to friends, but I hadn't believed it.

Thanks to Dana's persistence, I learned that I'm a valuable creation of God. Because of God I can build strong friendships. I can be a Dana to someone else.

I recognized that popularity isn't something I want in a friend after all.

The next day I saw this even more clearly. There was a

huge fight in the hall. It was mainly between Sandy and another girl. When Dana tried to stand up for the girl Sandy was yelling at, Sandy attacked Dana. Sandy accused Dana of something she didn't do, and then realized she was wrong. She apologized, but Dana was really hurt. I wasn't sure what to do. I figured I should stand up for her. But I worried they would attack me too. I didn't want that to happen so I kept quiet for a while. Finally I spoke up. Everything got quiet. My heart was in my throat. But I was glad I did what I did.

I realized I could give to Dana, just as she had given to me.

What Dana and I have is more than just standing up for each other. It's giving to each other in all kinds of ways. I'm more talkative, so I make it easier for quiet Dana to talk. Dana is more secure, so she frees me to worry less. I'm quick to forgive and Dana is quick to let things roll off her back, so we can help each other with problems. Together we bring out the best in each other.

God had given me friends, friends in response to the prayer I'd prayed. But I almost rejected them. Now that Dana, Karla, and I are friends, I wonder what I ever did without them. And even Teresa is starting to talk to me again.

This story is shorter than the other three for a reason:
Helping friends face down the tough stuff
boils down to simple friendship.
And yet you know friendship is not that simple.
The good news is you can make it simple
with actions like these:
• Hear each other's stories.
• Go places together and do life together.
• Say out loud the good you see in each other.

- Show the consideration you want from others.
  - Notice the people who treat you well,
    and spend more time with them.
- Realize the power of simple caring and genuine interest.

Even when middle school friendships get weird.
Even when labels like "popular" and
"dumb" get in the way.
You have the ability, because of Jesus,
to move past these obstacles
and grow friendships that
are deeper and truer
than any you've ever known.

It's your choice.

Daily look for a new way
to grow more caring;
to listen with more interest;
to have better fun;
to delight in the good and the beautiful.
Friendship, like any skill, grows better with practice.

Invite your parent or another trusted adult to show you
what you do well friend-wise,
and to teach you how you can get even better.

Be the friend who
smiles instead of rolls her eyes,
speaks instead of snubs,
cries along with rather than pushes away the pain,
laughs with people and never at them,
likes the people who are truly likable.

Treasure those who treasure God.
Value those who value people.
Love those who are free to be freely happy.
Go watch your friend in the play.
Go where your friend likes to go.
Go into even the hardest of settings simply
because your friend needs you.

Encourage those who choose ugly actions
to turn back to caring actions
simply by doing so yourself.
Give yourself a limited dose of ugly-acting people,
balanced with a big dose of people
who choose to turn outside themselves
and show faith in God through real friendship.

Be yourself and like yourself.
Invite God to make you and your friends
more like Him each day.
Jesus said it like this in John 15:15:
". . . I have called you friends,
for everything that I learned from my Father
I have made known to you."

Together, you and your friends can listen to God
and teach each other what you learn.
It's called fellowship,
and it's lived out with friendship actions that obey this
verse in Hebrews 10:25:
". . . encourage one another—
and all the more as you see the Day approaching."

That Day is the day when God will wipe away all that is

painful and bad.
Revelation 21:4 explains that He will personally
"wipe every tear from their eyes.
There will be no more death
or mourning
or crying
or pain,
for the old order of things has passed away."

One day you and your friend will have no more struggles
or pain,
but until then,
walk together with each other,
and with God,
through both the easy and the hard of life.
Enjoy the good, and treasure the simple.
Laugh at the happy,
and cry at the sad.
Because when you face life together,
you experience life as God means it to be.

Tools for the Tough Stuff

If you have a friendship challenge or know someone who
does, these sources can answer your questions or direct you
to someone who can:

• Listen to Christian music. Good lyrics can remind you
how to treat your friends, and how to thank them for the
good ways they treat you. Friendship tips from Christian
music include:

• Be there for each other ("Lean on Me" by DC Talk);

• Go through hard times together ("Go There with You"
by Steven Curtis Chapman);

• Show unity even during disagreements ("Friend Like U" by Geoff Moore & the Distance);

• Remind each other to spend your days well ("Seize the Day" by Carolyn Arends);

• Keep building a friendship ("Friends" by Michael W. and Deborah D. Smith).

Secular songs too often encourage getting each other back, betrayal, and selfishness. These are tempting moves, but they make things worse instead of better.

• Read your Bible. Look at the way people in Bible accounts treated each other. A few of the many verses that directly impact friendships include the book of Ruth; 1 Corinthians 13; Proverbs 15:1; 17:17; 18:24.

• Read Christian books such as Chariot Victor's Lights, Camera, Action Mysteries, TruthQuest, or Focus on the Family's China Tate Series. Let the kids in these stories give you ideas for solving your own friendship difficulties.

A NOTE TO PARENTS, TEACHERS, AND CAREGIVERS

You feel so bad for them.

Your nephew faces a learning disability and you wonder if he'll succeed at school.

The child you've liked since she was a preschooler has just been diagnosed with cancer at age eight.

Another divorce is breaking the heart of your daughter's best friend.

Your own child is reeling from a former friend's announcement that he's no longer cool enough to sit with the friends he's known since kindergarten.

You feel so bad. You'd do anything to take away their pain.

But feeling bad won't take away their pain. And trying to erase the pain with words like, "Everything will be okay," makes a child feel invisible.

So what's the answer? Walk with the child through her pain. Then equip her to manage the tough stuff she faces. It won't be easy, but it's a whole lot easier than abandoning a child to suffer alone.

Start by recognizing that the world of childhood is far from trouble-free. Learning disabilities, cancer, divorce, death, and damaged friendships haunt the happy days we want our children to have. We'd like to wish these away. We'd like to pretend they don't happen. But the tough stuff is reality. It's part of this imperfect world we live in (Rom. 8:19-21; Rev. 21:1-4). So face it down together. As you accompany your children through the pain, you become the vehicle through whom God shows His love. Children feel less lonely when they have a hand to hold. They feel God's very real hugs and very needed attention.

Continue by equipping your children to manage their crises. There are ways around every tough circumstance. So find those ways with God's help. Invite teachers and fellow parents to show you strategies that overcome your nephew's learning disability. Ask nurses for distractions during painful cancer treatments so your friend can get back to the fun of life. Teach relationship skills so kids can get along with new siblings in their blended families. List ten positive ways to respond to the cruel friends who insist on ugly words rather than encouraging ones.

In any tough experience assure children that their feelings make sense. Anger, confusion, and feeling betrayed are fitting responses to the tough stuff of this world. Give outlets for these powerful feelings so kids can face their tough stuff rather than be eaten alive.

As you hear children tell you their stories, it's okay to say, "I understand." You can't say, "I know how you feel," unless you've been through exactly the same experience. But you can listen closely enough to hear how that child feels about this experience this time.

Even when you haven't been through these things yourself, you can understand the feelings. You know what being sad, mad, worried, or confused feels like. Let your understanding of the feelings, combined with a willingness to listen to specific circumstances, provide the care your friend needs.

Finally, just enjoy children. Kids going through tough stuff are kids first. Help with the tough stuff, but don't stay there. Ask about things other than the learning disability, the cancer, the blended family, and the friendship squabble. Share the good stuff of life as well as the bad. And stick with each other through thick and thin, confident that life is worth living no matter the obstacles.

When you feel bad about a tough time a child is going through, let your sadness prompt you to loving action. No matter how personally painful it may be for you, willingly walk with your child through the pain. Refuse to abandon her to suffer or cope alone. Add your strength to his. Do the practical things that make a real difference. There is always something you can do to help.

The children in this book have shown you how.

IDEAS FOR GROUP OR INDIVIDUAL STUDY

Whether you're a child, parent, teacher, church worker, or another adult who cares about children, search this book for stories, questions, strategies, spiritual applications, and much more. Let the children show you how to face learning disabilities, serious illness, blended families, and friendship struggles.

Start with the M.I.N.I.S.T.R.Y. actions that launch this chapter. By putting feet on your care, you'll help all types of tough stuff.

Then move on to specific attitudes, dos/don'ts, and questions that match the four examples of tough stuff in this volume. Notice ways even the most specific actions might fit another area of tough stuff your young friend is walking through.

Make certain you hear. Rather than assume you know what your friend is thinking and feeling, invite your friend to tell you. Be the yearned-for friend or parent who wants

to hear the details. Questions that show your interest
include:
- Will you tell me about it?
- What's school like this year?
- What do you think about what's happening to you?
- What makes you so mad?
- What makes you happy and sad these days?
- How would you change things if you could?
- What actions have you tried to help with that problem?

*I*ncarnate the Word. Rather than just quote Scripture, live
it. As you give homework help, deliver kid-friendly meals,
do laundry, teach friendship skills, and keep hearing the
details, you show the Romans 8:28 good that God continues
to give even during crises. As you go along with your
friend to cancer treatments or therapy sessions, you show
the Romans 8:37-39 truth that God never abandons us. As
you accept every feeling including uncomfortable anger
and scary questions, you show the Ephesians 4:25-27 truth
that emotions point us to actions God wants us to take.

*N*otes are more great ways to contact between visits.
Sometimes visits are too intense during the height of the
tough stuff. So leave answering-machine messages, back-
door gifts, cookie bouquets, letters, coloring books, floss for
friendship bracelets, and more. You don't have to be there
in person to express God's love, but doing nothing makes a
family feel abandoned.

I can care no matter how much it hurts. Too many people
avoid children who are going through tough stuff because it
hurts them. They can't figure out why innocent children
have to go through such agonizing stuff. But when we

refuse to express care, children suffer alone. You can help kids face down the tough stuff because God will equip you (Phil. 4:13, 19) and because He Himself will one day wipe away all our tears (Rev. 21:4).

Show others how. Ephesians 4 reminds us that we are equippers to prepare God's people for works of service. Caring during tough stuff is one of these services. So mobilize a caring team in your church, made up of both kids and adults. Show them how to listen, befriend, walk together with simple words like, "This is Terry. Will you show him the ropes and let him sit by you during class?" or "Let's each wrap a gift for Jenny. Then she can open one each time she has a chemo treatment." Help your team accept tears as signs of love (John 11:35-36). Prompt them to be strong by sharing the pain rather than pushing it away (Rom. 12:15). Show them how to give the practical help kids need, such as some privacy, some company, help with homework, invitations to events, lack of labels, and more (Matt. 25:31-46).

Teach kids about it. Children are often cruel when they don't understand. When a nurse came to explain Emily's cancer fight, her fourth-grade classmates said things like, "Why will her hair fall out?" and "My cat had leukemia and it died." The nurse was able to explain that the hair falls out because chemo goes after fast-growing cells and hair is one of the fastest growing. She also explained that, though cats die of leukemia, kids usually survive. This group of children then took up for Emily when a child in another class, who did not know about Emily's cancer, made fun of her hat. They educated other children. They demonstrated that as children understand they show care. Invite the parents, teachers, medical professionals, and others to tell you what they want you to know and what they'd like you to do. Be a good gossip by spreading the word.

*R*emember. Mark on your calendar the day of the learning challenge, the date of cancer diagnosis, the remarriage date, the friendship pain, the birth, death, and more. Then give care in the form of a card, a call, a personal touch: "I'm praying with you as the proficiency tests approach." For continuing crises, repeat the care in two weeks, two months, one year, and annually after that. "I remember that your baby sister died this month, and I want you to know that she and you matter to me."

*Y*ou really love the child rather than feel sorry for him or her. Kids going through tough stuff don't want to be set apart, admired, or treated with kid gloves. They want to be loved. So cuddle, listen to, and enjoy them. See them as the delightful individuals they are, and equip them to give as well as receive.

IMPORTANT: Hurting kids are not heroes; they feel lonely and isolated. Refuse to isolate them more by putting them on a spiritual pedestal or admiring them from the pulpit. This urges church members to feel different from them and hesitate to approach them with normal friendship. Instead, teach your church members to live Romans 12:15 and John 11:35-36 with concrete expressions of care, by hurting along with them, and by giving practical help.

Learning Disabilities

When your friend has a learning disability:
• Avoid any references to being dumb or retarded, even

in jest. In fact, don't use these terms at all; someone near you struggles with a learning difference or knows someone who does.

• Remember that you and your friend are more alike than different—you both want to be seen as smart; you both want to do well in school.

• Notice ways your friend is smart, and tell her what you notice.

• Casually but firmly stop any taunting or joking about "dumb classes" or special education by using one-sentence reminders that everyone is smart in unique ways.

• Show each other the strategies you use to study, play sports, and do the stuff of life. Sharing life is how friendships grow.

• Sometimes just study, practice sports, and do life stuff without teaching each other. Just do it.

Dos and Don'ts

Do treat all kids like human beings and value what they say.	Don't equate gifted with smart and learning disabled with dumb. All kids have ways they learn well and learn poorly; all kids have new information to learn. Especially during Bible studies, show that all kids are on equal footing.
Do work together to find ways to hurdle learning barriers and make learning enjoyable.	Don't assume you have to do all the giving. Your friend with a learning disability is smart and wise in ways you are not. Learn from him or her.

Do trust God for strategies to learn.	Don't assume God gave some people less ability to learn. Instead assume that God struggles when we struggle, and that God will give us strategies, friends, and teachers to help. "For God is not a God of disorder but of peace" (1 Cor. 14:33). God gives good gifts, not frustration. He will help until the learning difficulties pass away with all the other imperfections of this world (1 John 1:5; Rom. 8:19).
Do make each other feel capable by involving each person in every aspect of Bible study at church.	Don't assume that because reading is difficult the student doesn't want to read aloud. Instead, ask privately if it's okay to call on her. Then let her be a part of things.
Do laugh *with* kids, not *at* them. Laugh about all kinds of stuff rather than make people the brunt of jokes.	Don't laugh at jokes about ANY person. Refuse ever to ridicule or taunt a person for any reason.
Do help each other understand without feeling set apart or put on the spot.	Don't forget to let friends with learning disabilities help others in the group understand. Let all members give and all members receive.

Do accept all feel-ings including anger, confusion, and sadness.	Don't just hear feelings. Find out what to do with them. Invite an adult friend or parent to help as Katie did. Sometimes just saying feelings out loud makes them manageable. Other times, action is needed.

Questions for Facing Down the Tough Stuff Together

1. How does God want you to be a friend like Kimberly, Kathryn's friend? Kathryn said this about her: "She said, '[your learning disability] didn't make any difference. . . When we met, I could tell you had a lot of talent and were very smart. You are the most talented artist I know.'"

2. What actions do you take at your church to intentional-ly include each student, to make church "a place where I don't have to worry about my learning disability"?

3. Everybody is smart in his or her own way. Think of ten people from your family, school, church, and neighborhood. How is each smart? How will you compliment them for being smart this way?

4. If you're an adult, how will this paragraph impact your teaching at church or school: "Teachers seem to think I'll burst from the pressure if they assign me a science experi-ment or essay, but I'd like to try. . . . Mrs. Williams once gave me a poetry assignment, and I loved it. What kids like us need is to be treated like normal students. We want all the interesting learning that other classes have. We want teachers to respect us as people, not as abnormalities, cases, inferior students, or as people who aren't capable of cre-ative learning. When teachers respect us, we'll give it back. And when we respect teachers, they seem to respect us. We can work together."

5. God promises to equip us for all things, according to

passages such as Philippians 4:13 and 4:19. How would each of these strategies help you or your friend learn?

- Listen with your eyes as well as your ears.
- Write on a computer instead of by hand.
- Underline in the book you're reading.
- Picture the fact, page, or topic in your mind.
- Study with a friend.
- Draw the fact/topic as a picture on paper.
- Do math problems on graph paper to keep columns in rows.
- Read out loud (at home).
- Partner up with a good note taker and give each other copies of your notes.
- Learn with learning games.
- Make a to-do list in order of importance and then use the to-do list.
- Write assignments so you won't forget them.
- Recheck work.
- Tape record the class and play back at home.
- Sing math facts.
- Study by speaking the content into a tape recorder.
- Ask until you understand.
- Make a crossword puzzle or word search with spelling or vocabulary words.
- While writing, tape your paper to the table to keep it in place.
- Use memory codes such as: N.ever E.at S.our W.ater-melon for N.orth, E.ast, S.outh, W.est.
- Tell someone what you learned (talking helps you remember).
- Hang good papers on the refrigerator to remind yourself you can do well.

6. How could you offer one of the above strategies with-

out making your friend feel dumb?

7. Tell about a time you labeled someone or heard someone labeled. How did it cause you and others to treat that person?

8. Why is a person's name the best label of all?

9. Learning disabilities and other problems can make us mad. The Bible says to "be angry" but "not let your anger lead you into sin" (Eph. 4:26, GNB). How do you get mad without sinning? (Examples include: Talk about your anger to someone who cares; use a mediator; hit a punching bag or do other physical activity; write a letter that you never mail; talk with the person who made you angry to ask for a change; draw or sing about your feelings; pray or read a favorite Bible passage).

10. How will you show friendship to someone who differs from you in school ability? (Ideas include: assume we're more alike than different; listen and understand; talk to every person without feeling higher or lower than anybody; point out areas in which we agree; grow close to people who are kind . . . but be nice to everyone; talk about feelings rather than be moody; bring out the best in each other).

Serious Illnesses

When your friend has a serious illness:

• Expect some angry and confused feelings. Anger and confusion are good reactions to your friend's suffering—just direct your anger and confusion to the devil who deserves both. Ask God your questions until you find the answers.

• Remember that you're more alike than different—you both would rather be well than sick.

• Refuse to assume that this illness came so your friend could grow closer to God. Your friend feels too sick to grow.

Instead she will lean on God and the faith she has built up to now. She will let God hug her.

• Find ways to play even during the illness. Can you go to the play room together or do something fun in the hospital room? Ask your friend, her parents, and her doctors for ideas.

• Let your friend guide the way. If he wants to talk, talk. If he wants to be quiet, be quiet. If he wants to tell the details of the illness, listen. If he's mad, be mad together. If he's glad, be glad together.

• Do the stuff of life together around the cancer fight. Play piano duets to distract from chemotherapy pain. Invite your friend over. Be in each other's group at school. Find out what's safe to do and do it.

Dos and Don'ts

Do find out what your friend and his or her family need, and then do those things. Does your friend need you to take notes at school? To keep him up on what's happening at church? To visit? To send fun gifts? To laugh with him?

Don't forget to keep doing those things that are needed. Write them on your calendar and enlist other friends to help you.

Do trust God to help you and your friend every step of the way.	Don't assume God sent the illness. Don't say things like, "God won't give us more than we can bear." This misquotes 1 Corinthians 10:13. The verse is actually about temptation, not troubles.
Do ask questions directly to the person or the family.	Don't ask other people what the person herself knows best. By asking directly you get correct information, and your friend knows you care about details.
Do learn about the illness, including asking doctors and nurses how to help.	Don't read any literature that's more than five years old. Advances in treating cancer and other serious illnesses mean more kids survive and thrive each year.
Do find out whether the illness is contagious.	Don't fear catching cancer or disabilities. They aren't contagious. But do protect yourself from contagious illnesses. And do guard your ill friend from getting your bugs. Chicken pox and other "small" sicknesses can be deadly to someone with certain illnesses. Stay away if you've been exposed, since the day before your break out is the most contagious.
Do assure that your friend has the best possible medical treatment.	Don't allow doctors to simply use your child or your friend as a guinea pig.

Do be a source of blessing by coming over to play, by getting notes at school, by taping conversations with friends, and by keeping your friend in touch with life while he's at home or in the hospital.	Don't ever call cancer, or MS or any illness a blessing. Illnesses distort the very good way God made our bodies. Rather than talking about blessings, be one.
Do accept all feelings, including anger, confusion, and sadness.	Don't assume you know how your friend feels. Let him tell you when and how he wants to. Just saying feelings out loud makes them easier to manage.

Questions for Facing Down the Tough Stuff Together

1. How does God want you to be a friend like Mary, Emily's friend? Emily said this about her:

"Mom picked up Mary on the way to the hospital. . . . Knowing I had a spinal ahead . . . I acted kind of crazy, but Mary didn't let my nervousness bother her. We just kept playing cards. . . . [After my spinal and] on the way home I was pretty quiet. Relief that it was over plus getting up so early had me pretty tired. Mary didn't make me talk. She just sat next to me while we listened to [Christian music]. When we got to my house, we played piano duets. The music distracted me from the pain. . . . it was back to school on Monday. Mary met me outside my classroom. She knew I wouldn't feel well, but she didn't worry about it. She didn't push me, but she also didn't let me stay on the side-lines and feel sorry for myself. 'C'mon, Emily. Be my partner for this science experiment.' she urged. There's a verse in the Bible that says to put your love into action. Mary does that for me."

2. Emily found out about her cancer at a hospital. Have you ever been really sick? What places, sounds, and smells do you remember?

3. Illnesses come from this imperfect world, not from God. How does God help you fight illnesses?

4. In addition to Himself, God gives friends, parents, siblings, doctors, and nurses as part of your fighting team. How have they helped you get better? How have they helped you even when you didn't get better?

5. What are some fun things to take along when you visit a friend in the hospital?

6. Emily was glad to get back to school and church. How has a daily routine helped you with your illness?

7. Which of these ways have you or could you help a friend during illness? Which would you like someone to do for you?

- Get school assignments and books.
- Go along to a doctor's appointment.
- Ask how it's going, and really listen.
- Send a card, letter, gift.
- Spend time together.
- Pray for specific concerns.
- Ask your friend to explain her illness.
- Read books or articles about it.
- Bring your friend's favorite food.
- Do a chore for your friend.
- For a long illness, buy and wrap a series of gifts and tell your friend to open one a day.

• If she has to be in the hospital, make a tape of lots of people talking to her.

• Keep visiting, calling, and writing even if your friend misses a lot of school.

8. Illness is only one part of life. What do you like about the other parts of your life? How do you go on living even in the face of pain or death?

9. Who has your illness or an illness like it? How do you encourage and help each other?

10. What do you most look forward to about heaven where God will erase all illnesses and handicaps? (Rev. 21:4-5).

Blended Families

When your friend has gone through divorce, death of a parent, or a blended family:

• Avoid assuming that your family is whole and your friend's family is broken. Focus instead on the actions *all* families must take to be close: mutual appreciation, listening, problem solving, kindness, getting along.

• Remember that you're more alike than different—you both want to be happy in your families.

• Understand the complexity of the relationships. You may find it hard to remember who is the parent and who is the stepparent. That's okay. Ask questions. Privately make a chart. Then grow in understanding by hearing your friend's experiences with each family member.

• Invite your friend to tell what he likes about his family.

• Show the love, grace, and mercy of God by treating your friend as valuable and interesting.

• Notice and use the power of choice. If all family members said nice words only when they felt like it, a lot more families would break up. If all family members chose kind words and actions no matter how they felt, many more families would be close.

Dos and Don'ts

Do listen again each time your friend wants to talk about her family.

But don't assume every problem your friend has is related to her family. Help each other out with all kinds of struggles.

Do agree that divorce is destructive because it hurts kids, their parents, and everyone who knows those kids and parents.

But don't set divorce up as the unpardonable sin. All sin is destructive. And all separation hurts. So avoid the two extremes of divorce reaction: (1) Divorce is no big deal; and (2) Only undivorced families are good. Like Jesus, love the people and find ways to do good in the present circumstances (Eph. 4:32).

Do recognize that we all make mistakes and we can all help each other through them.

But don't assume that divorce pain is no big deal. Instead, communicate togetherness: Together we can find God's healing for the pain we all feel. Together each of us can grow closer to the plan God has for us.

Do spend time at your friends' houses and invite them to yours.

Don't assume that only one kind of family is good. Instead, learn from the strengths and weaknesses in all families.

Do invite God's help for blending into a new family.	Don't accept wrong behaviors of other family members. Instead, persistently but kindly work for right.
Do see the strengths in each of your friends' family members.	Don't assume the stepparents and stepsiblings are better or worse.
Do accept all feelings, including anger, confusion, and sadness.	Don't be afraid to let your friend talk about his or her feelings, even the lousy ones. Any feeling is okay; some actions are not.

Questions for Facing Down the Tough Stuff Together

1. What do you think is God's secret to living happily with a blended family?

2. Families are built, not born. Tell about how you see this in at least one blended family and in one family that has lived together without a remarriage.

3. People who study stepfamilies say it takes an average of five years for a blended family to feel like a family. How have you seen this in your family, or in the family of someone you know?

4. What makes each of your parents easy to get along with? Hard? When are you hard to get along with? What do you do to make yourself easy to get along with?

5. On a scale of 1-10 with 10 being perfectly easy to manage, how easy do you find each of these emotions in your family: Sadness? Love? Anger? Fear? Wonder? Worries? Confusion? Hope?

6. You alone can't fix your family, because each family

member chooses to create or squash happiness. But you can create some happiness. How will you create happiness in your family?

• Listen to my parents' and siblings' opinions, trying to understand why they feel as they do.

• Be considerate by taking turns in the bathroom, taking turns talking, and so on.

• Speak with kindness even when I feel cross.

• Notice and say what I agree with.

• Sincerely compliment other family members.

• Share dreams.

• Hear and cherish the dreams of other family members.

• Tell about my day.

• Hear with interest the daily events of my parents, brothers, and sisters.

• Express emotions calmly.

• Explain why I feel as I do.

• Treat my sisters and brothers well.

• Be happy with those who are happy and weep with those who weep (Rom. 12:15).

• Do the caring thing even when I don't feel like it.

• Try to understand mean actions rather than automatically react.

• Tell good stories about each family member (never ridiculing with these stories).

7. How would doing each of the above help you to help a friend create happiness in his or her family?

8. What do you do to make it through your sad and mad times? (Examples: think it through; talk it out; write it down; sing a song; hear good music; read the Bible; make a poster; understand the meaning—all with God's help).

9. God likes some things that happen in your family and doesn't like other things. What does He want you to imitate

in your family? To change to something else?

10. What do you remember about your parents' divorce or death? Remarriage? What questions do you still have? Whom will you ask?

11. Anna in the story says it's hard to know lifetime love if you've never experienced it. Kids whose parents have divorced are more likely to divorce. But lifetime love is still possible because love is a choice (choose to be kind, choose to listen, choose to be considerate, choose to see the way things really are rather than how you want them to be, and so on). Whom do you know who has been married several years and is still in love? How will you imitate their love with deliberate choices?

12. Many things can change but one thing never changes: God won't divorce you, move away from you, or hurt you. He will always understand you, stay with you, help you, teach you. How have you experienced this security?

Friendship Squabbles

When your friend has a friendship struggle:

• Hear all the details before you give advice.

• Ask more questions than you give answers. Your friend will tend to blame you if your advice doesn't work. It is better to ask questions that guide your friend to think things over and choose his or her own conclusion.

• Remember that you're more alike than different—you both have good times and bad times with friends

• Refuse to take sides. Instead, voice the good in every person and the possible reasons for each action.

• Show your care by speaking to every person and valuing every person.

• Be the kind of friend you want others to be to you.

• Consistently be a caring and steady friend by obeying these words in Ephesians 4:29, 31-32: "Do not let any unwholesome talk come out of your mouths, but only what is helpful for building others up according to their needs, that it may be*nefit those who listen. . . .* Get rid of all bitterness, rage and anger, brawling and slander, along with every form of malice. Be kind and compassionate to one another. . . ."

Dos and Don'ts

Do assure kids that the middle school years are the hardest.	Don't allow them to mope over it. Instead, give them skills to solve each problem as it comes up.
Do recognize that every person in middle school is going through the angst of adolescence, and so is more touchy and harder to get along with.	But don't excuse cruel or rejecting behavior. Let it prompt greater efforts for kindness.
Do stress daily discipleship: obeying God in everyday life.	Don't bless kids who talk the talk, but then act cruelly at church and at school. A startling majority of Christian kids have mastered this charade.
Do refuse to call friendship	Don't make relationship mountains out of daily molehills. Instead, let each inci-

problems smaller than learning disabilities, cancer, or death. Instead, see it as a widespread problem that impacts every area of life.

dent focus you and your friend on learning critical skills such as negotiation, honest but kind expression of feelings, commitment to friendship rather than fads, and ultimately the truth that God will provide for your needs. Find courage to be yourself so you and your friends can find kindred spirits. Remind each other that if one friend abandons you, other friends will choose to care. God will prompt this caring (Phil. 4:19).

Do be a friend rather than just waiting for others. Someone has to make the first moves. Let it be you.

Don't let people trample you; instead choose friends who value you in return (Matt. 7:6).

Do accept all feelings, including anger, confusion, and sadness

Don't dwell on sad feelings. This causes you to miss the good. Be just as eager to talk about the good friendship feelings like success, togetherness, belonging, and friendship.

Questions for Facing Down the Tough Stuff Together
1. How does God want you to be a friend like Dana, Elizabeth's friend? Elizabeth said this about her: "I couldn't think of one time she had put me down. I like that. . . . Dana's lunch table [had] a difference in tone. . . . People still

said insulting things. But the insults were occasional rather than constant. And people often apologized—'Oops. I shouldn't have said it that way.' Could Dana be the reason? People seemed to know she cared."

2. Why do friendships change so drastically in middle school?

3. Which middle-school changes are the way God wants them? Which are not?

4. Insults and put-downs are a big part of our society. But they are still destructive. Why?

5. With what words and actions do you refuse insults? (Examples: deliberately compliment, translate cuts before they come out of my mouth, close my mouth before they can get out.)

6. If we all need friends so badly, why are we so cruel to each other?

7. Why does the popularity myth have pull?

8. Talk about a friend who pulled away from you. What did you do about it? How would God advise you to respond next time?

9. When can this be said about you: "I'm pushing away a totally nice person just because I'm worried about what other people think." How will God help you push away the feeling, rather than the friend?

10. Tell about a time you experienced this, or created it for someone else: *"This is what friendship feels like,* I recognized. Friendship is supposed to be fun and crazy times with people you really like and who like you back."

11. With what actions will you build even more experiences like those in #10?

- Listen to people and really care about what they think.
- Treat every person well.
- Value honesty, kindness, and fun.

- Let God make me comfortable being myself.
- Point out the good in my friends.
- Believe the good they see in me.
- Help my friends through rough times.
- Remind myself that I'm lovable.
- Notice friends who really like me, not just pretend to like me.
- Notice the good that God made in me.
- Share special things together.
- Remember what my friend says.
- Feel both sad and happy together.
- Be sensitive to feelings.
- Refuse to make fun of anyone.
- Stand up for people.
- Have genuine fun together rather than worry about fads or "supposed tos."
- Do the actions in 1 Corinthians 13.

12. We can't solve every problem in our friendships. That's because some friends make choices that we cannot change. How does God help you with unfixable friendships?

Two Closing Tips

Tip #1- Give copies of this book to children you know, whether they're going through tough stuff or not. Then when they do go through tough times, they'll have more tools to manage. And when a friend goes through tough times, he or she can offer friendship and understanding.

Tip #2-Never use a child in crisis to make yourself or your children feel better. Ponder for a moment the impact of statements such as: "Kids like this make me grateful for my own kids," and "I just visit a children's hospital to make my problems seem small."

At the very least it's selfish—you're focusing on yourself rather than the one who needs you. At the very most it adds more pain to the child—the pain of isolation and being different. You don't mean to hurt anyone, but when you use suffering people to make yourself feel better, you separate yourself from the very children who need you. You cruelly assume that God let these children go through troubles to help you count your blessings. You don't want to hurt anyone. So avoid this very destructive pattern. Rather than thinking, "I'm glad I'm not in that circumstance," push your thoughts to, "What would I want if I were in this circumstance?" Then give the care you'd want.

Look for these and other exciting products from Chariot Victor...

Truth Quest Series
by Tad Hardy

Rachel and her cousin Elliot encounter mysterious people and discover many exciting things as they travel on archeological digs in faraway places. Ages 8-12.

THE MOUNTAIN THAT BURNS WITHIN
ISBN: 0-78143-001-1
TREASURE OF THE HIDDEN TOMB
ISBN: 0-78143-003-8
THE VALLEY OF THE GIANTS
ISBN: 0-78143-002-X

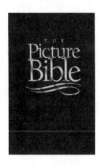

THE PICTURE BIBLE

The Picture Bible makes a good first Bible for young readers, though this classic best-seller is loved by people of all ages. The full-text version contains 266 Bible stories in full-color comic format that makes Bible stories exciting for kids. Newly revised, the new information pages, maps, and improved indexes give this classic Bible storybook fresh significance for today!

DELUXE HARDCOVER	ISBN: 0-78143-057-7
PAPERBACK	ISBN: 0-78143-058-5
HARDCOVER	ISBN: 0-78143-055-0
THE NEW TESTAMENT	ISBN: 0-78143-056-9

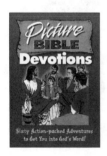

PICTURE BIBLE DEVOTIONS
Edited by Jeannie Harmon

ISBN: 0-78143-067-4

Interactive activities and full-color pictures from *The Picture Bible* make this an innovative approach to devotions. Kids learn to apply Bible knowledge to their lives through 30 Old Testament and 30 New Testament stories.

GRANDMA'S ATTIC SERIES
by Arleta Richardson

American life around the turn of the century is the
backdrop for these heart-warming, real-life stories!
And while some things have changed for young girls.
some haven't–like friendship, looking good, sibling
rivalry, boys, competition, and Christian Values.
Ages 8-12.

IN GRANDMA'S ATTIC
ISBN: 0-78140-085-6
MORE STORIES FROM GRANDMA'S ATTIC
ISBN: 0-78140-086-4
STILL MORE STORIES FROM GRANDMA'S ATTIC
ISBN: 0-78140-087-2
TREASURES FROM GRANDMA
ISBN: 0-78140-088-0

SARAH'S JOURNEY
by Wanda Luttrell

Exciting adventures in the life of Sarah Moore and her family reveal what life was really like for pioneers in the time of Daniel Boone and the American Revolution. Historically accurate fiction skillfully blended with true-to-life characters and fast-paced action creates an adventure to be enjoyed by young and old alike. Ages 8 and up.

HOME ON STONEY CREEK
ISBN: 0-78140-901-2
STRANGER IN WILLIAMSBURG
ISBN: 0-78140-902-0
REUNION IN KENTUCKY
ISBN: 0-78140-907-1
SHADOWS ON STONEY CREEK
ISBN: 0-78143-005-4
WHISPERS IN WILLIAMSBURG
ISBN: 0-78143-008-9